Ghetto Diva

—REVISED EDITION—

Brandy Lerue

Written and created by: Brandy Lerue

Editor, Cover Design, and Interior Layout Design:
Devoe Publications

ISBN-13: 978-1-7368348-1-7

Published by: Unseen Pen Pusher

Acknowledgements

Before I acknowledge anyone, I must give praise and honor to God. Always consistent, will never leave or forsake me, always have my back, and will guide me through any situation. Without him, neither I nor this book would be possible. To him I give all the glory.

To my #1 fans and biggest supporters, my children who are now grown, JeMari and Kenya. I must say, I have been blessed with some smart, creative, and decent kids. This world is big enough for you two to conquer any dream your hearts desire. Remember to always keep God first and everything else will fall into its proper prospective. My parents Rufus (Ruff Dogg) and Linda Johnson. I cherish and enjoy every moment I spend with y'all. My sidekick, my kidada, my partner in crime, my baby sister Fab, a.k.a. Ms. Fabulous. You know I love you to the moon and back. My niece Madison, your mom had you, but you're my baby. My oldest sisters Shaun and Tara. My voices of reasons. I love y'all to pieces. All my brothers, a.k.a. my protectors, Lafayette, Kraig and Lamont. All my nieces and nephews. It's a whole lot of y'all, but I'm gonna take a shot at it. If I forget someone, I owe you lunch. Madison Marie, Brittney, Poppa, Amber, Lil Lafayette 1 and Lil Lafayette 2, Unique (Ne Ne) Travonti, Tasha, William, Anaiya, Kylan, Logan, and Lyndon. I'm gonna be buying some lunch because I know I forgot a few. Auntie getting older, charge it to my brain and not my heart. My auntie Machele Burgess Williams…I don't know where to start. I've been looking up to you since I was a kid. You've talked me through some hard and rough times, talked me out of doing dumb stuff, thumped me upside my head and asked me, "What is wrong with you?" (I'm laughing out loud) God clearly speaks through you. I will always love and respect you. My best friend Jamila Reese and my sister best friend Alisha Reese, I love and appreciate you two. Y'all my dogs! My best friend Janet, a.k.a. Beauty. From hustling to make ends meet to success…all money in! I love how our conversations have transitioned over the years.

To my late husband Ronald. I think about you all day every single day. Your unexpected passing is still fresh, which means I am still crying every day, and you hated when I cry. I can hear you saying through clenched teeth, "Girl, you DO NOT cry." So, I'm going to keep this short and simple and try not to. I never imagined life without you. We were in a fun and functioning marriage which made the definition of forever seem like a million years away. I feel like what was promised to me was snatched away way too soon. It is still unreal! I will never stop loving you and I miss you like crazy.

Like everything I write, this is dedicated to my grandmother Jimmie Lee Wright, my auntie Myris, and now my husband Ronald. I love and miss you all so much.

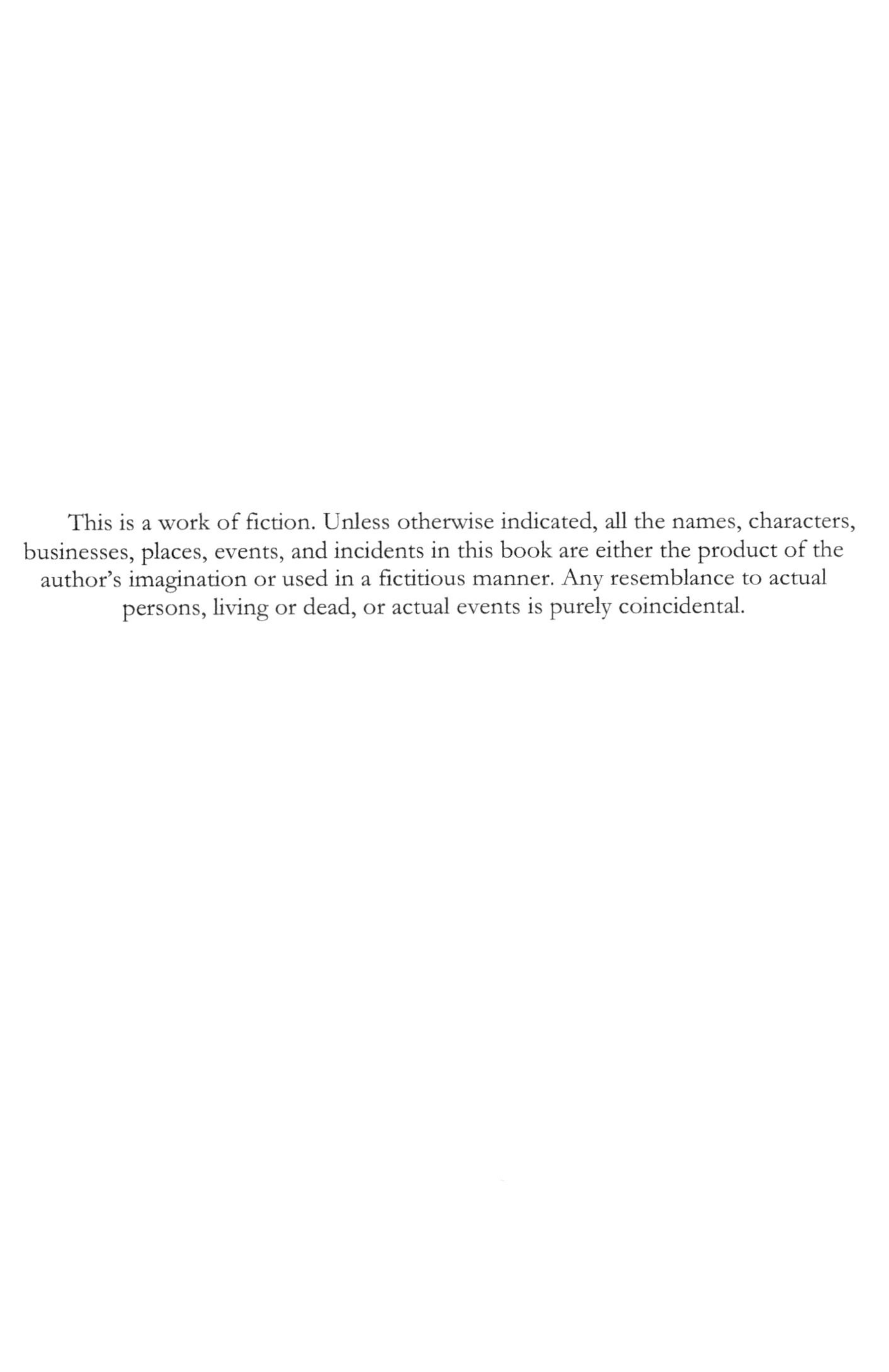

Chapter 1

Ugh! No this muthafucka didn't just sock me in my stomach! As soon as I catch my breath and unfold, I'ma fuck his ass up! Nestaja thought as she struggled, pulling herself from the floor while shaking off the blow she had just taken to the stomach from Reggie.

"Bitch, I been havin' a fucked up feelin' in my stomach all week. Now you need to feel some pain. Who you fuckin'? And I know it's somebody, cuz it ain't me. You like dick too much to not get none. So tell me, Nestaja?"

"I'm not messing with nobody, and if I was, I wouldn't tell you. Look how you are acting right now," Nestaja moaned. She tried to catch her breath and remain calm without their two children, Josiah and Jasmine, becoming suspicious of another physical altercation going on in the bedroom.

Reggie didn't care. As long as he got his point across and a few punches in, he was cool. "Bitch, give me your cell phone. I'm gon' find out who you been giving that pussy to."

"Nigga, I ain't givin' you shit," she sarcastically responded while coughing up everything she had eaten that day, spitting it directly into Reggie's face while swinging like she was in a boxing ring with her worst enemy. Even though Nestaja knew she couldn't win, this was one time she was going to give her all and leave some type of signature that she was there. As they continued to rumble and rearrange the room, Reggie grabbed Nestaja by the neck, slamming her into the floor. He took a deep plunge into her nose with his teeth, saying in a violent, enraged tone, "Bitch, if I can't have you, I be damned if anotha nigga do!"

Nestaja tried to loosen his grip by pulling his hand away from her neck. He had such a tight hold on her that she only became weaker and weaker. Due to lack of air, she started to slowly fade out. Reggie noticed her fight was suddenly coming to a halt. Once he loosened his grip, it appeared obvious to him that she was unresponsive. "Nestaja!" he yelled her name. "Nestaja!" he yelled again while shaking her. "Stop faking, 'cause you not getting no sympathy from me." Still, she didn't budge. "Nestaja!"

What have I done? he thought. This was not the first time Reggie had choked her out, but this was the first time she didn't respond. "God, please don't let this bitch be dead," Reggie prayed, hoping he hadn't killed her.

The children began banging on the door, screaming at the top of their lungs. "Mommy, open the door! Are you okay?"

They continued to bang and scream with desperation, wanting to hear that their mom was okay. Nestaja slowly began to move to the sound of their voices, attempting to respond to them. Once Reggie saw her movement, he blew a sigh of relief, but he didn't let up one bit. She tried to regain focus and shake it off as she made an attempt to get up and head for the door to comfort Josiah and Jasmine, only to get snatched back by her hair.

"Nigga, what the fuck?" Nestaja yelled. "Don't you hear the kids out there cryin', fool?

They scared!" she yelled.

"Bitch, you ain't goin' out there with a bloody nose like that! They gon' think I'm in here beatin' yo' ass."

"You are!" she replied.

She tried to force her way out the door, but Reggie grabbed the knob, slamming the door on her fingers. She turned around, pounding her knee into his nuts, causing him to fold over, which gave her full access to the door to comfort her children. First, she went into the kitchen and grabbed a towel, filling it with ice and applying it to her nose. Then she sat down on the couch to comfort Josiah and Jasmine.

"Mommy, what happened to your nose?" Jasmine asked.

But before Nestaja could respond, Reggie stormed out of the

room, saying, "Nothing, baby, you know Mommy is clumsy. She fell again."

Jasmine was fine with what her dad told her. She was just an innocent five-year-old girl. But Josiah wasn't buying it. He was twelve, and he knew what was going on. He slid his mom a note without Reggie noticing that read: *Mommy, I called the police, Auntie Asia, and Craz. And I left the front door unlocked so they can come in and get Reggie.* Reggie wasn't Josiah's biological father, but he was the only father figure in his life. Josiah loved and respected him, but he didn't like the fact that Reggie was so abusive to his mother.

"Don't you think you need to be doing something in the room?" Reggie demanded.

"I'm doing just what I'm supposed to be doing: sitting here with my kids and trying to stop my nose from bleeding."

"Nestaja, I just want to talk."

"There's nothing to be talked about unless it's about you getting your shit out my house. As a matter of fact, that's exactly what we're about to do: pack your shit, cuz you gettin' outta here today. I've suffered too many black eyes, busted lips, and contusions since I been with you. I don't know what you got goin' on, but lately you been acting like you usin' the products you sell. Your demeanor has changed drastically."

When Nestaja got up and headed to the room, the kids tried to come with her in hopes there wouldn't be another fight and that Reggie would just get his things and go. But he told them to stay in the living room because he and Mommy needed to talk. Once she entered the room with Reggie following behind damn near on her heels, he slammed the door shut, grabbed her by the collar, and slammed her against the wall, saying in a perverted, demanding tone,

"Bitch, strip and give me some pussy."

"Nigga, you have really lost your damn mind! I'm not giving you shit. Only thing you can get from me is a trash bag to put your lil trinkets in so you can roll up outta here."

He continued to push himself on her, but she fought like she was fighting for her innocence. Since he was stronger than she was, he was able to get her in a position so she couldn't move. He started snatching off her clothes, slapping her around, and demanding that she have sex with him.

BOOM!

An unexpected force pushed the bedroom door open, and there stood Nestaja's sister Asia and their friend Monique with pistols in hand.

"Nigga, get off my sister before you get flat-lined in this muthafucka!" Asia yelled.

Reggie's attitude suddenly changed, knowing the type of females Asia, Monique, and even Nestaja were when they were in a battle, so he began to turn everything on Nestaja. "See how your sister and homegirl just bust in our house like it's theirs? You need to be checkin' these bitches, baby."

Nestaja ignored his obtuse statement and that's when Reggie started to realize he wasn't too successful at turning the tables. He also realized he was slipping, since he had left his burner in his truck on the floor of the passenger seat, not thinking he would need it. He became furious on the inside but tried to stay hood and not let them see that he didn't want any problems. He wasn't expecting things to go this way. Asia had her burner in hand ready to bust. Monique was gangbanging on him and swinging her stiletto, hitting him in his head and upper torso, and since Nestaja was siding with her loved ones, Reggie knew he was outdone. The only thing left for him to do was surrender and try to make his way to his truck. Nestaja, not really wanting anything to happen to her baby daddy, spared his life by talking Asia into putting the gun down. Reggie quickly started to grab the bags that were packed but while doing so, the sounds of his alarm going off on his truck diverted his attention. He stepped out of the house to see what was going on and to his surprise, there stood Craz, Nestaja's new beau, standing with Reggie's own Mossberg pointed at his temple.

Nestaja ran out of the house screaming, "Baby, no, let him live, he ain't worth it!"

"Hell no, Nestaja, this nigga got me fucked up. You ain't his bitch no mo'. You with me now, and he dissin' me by puttin' his hands on you. Fuck this nigga!"

"Baby, please don't! Even though I can't stand his ass, he's my baby daddy, so give him a pass," Nestaja begged while giving Reggie the evil eye.

Craz loved Nestaja a great deal. She could pretty much persuade him to do just about anything, so he slowly uncocked the gun. Just as he began to lower it, a loud screeching sound approaching them grabbed everyone's attention. Seeing it was the police hitting the block, Monique acted fast. She took the burner from Craz, tucked it in her purse, and walked away without being noticed. Asia slid inside to tuck everything away in the house. Thank God Josiah had taken Jasmine into the back room to watch cartoons and they weren't exposed to all the chaos going on. The police hit the block seven cars deep, jumping out with guns in hand.

"Everybody put your hands up where I can see them and don't fucking move!"

Since the police in L.A. were known for brutality and being assholes and no one wanted any problems, everybody did as they were told.

"Is anyone on probation or parole?" one officer asked.

Craz and Reggie were both on parole, so they both answered yes.

"Any guns or drugs we should know about before we do any searching?" "No!" they all replied.

"Whose house is this?" "Mine," Nestaja answered.

"Is anyone inside?" the officer asked. "Yes, my sister and my children."

"I'm gonna need you to step over here with me," the officer demanded. "Hello, I'm Officer Waters, and we received two calls saying there was some commotion going on involving a gun," he stated.

"Me and my baby daddy had a lil argument." "Was there a gun involved?"

"Naw!" she responded.

"Are there any weapons inside the house?" "Nope!" she answered nonchalantly.

"May I see some identification, please?" "It's in my car, let me grab it for you." "Sure!" he responded.

Before Nestaja could turn and walk away, Officer Waters noticed the bleeding cut on her nose. "What happened?" he asked

"I was tryna leave to avoid an argument. I obviously was moving too fast, 'cause I tripped on my front porch causing me to fall into the rail and hit my nose."

"Can I get you a paramedic? That cut looks pretty deep."

"Naw, I'm good!" she rudely answered.

When she headed to her car to get her driver's license, she started to pray that he didn't run her name and see the numerous traffic violations she had accumulated and kept putting off. She couldn't see herself going to jail for some minor traffic tickets that could have been avoided.

She got her driver's license out of her car. As she handed it to the officer, she noticed how attractive he was. He stood about 6'2" tall with a smooth mocha complexion. He was very muscular with a clean bald head and some sexy bedroom brown eyes. He also had many stripes on his uniform, meaning he had rank and he wasn't a rookie. When Nestaja noticed his appearance, her demeanor changed. She started talking proper as if she was on a job interview. That was one of her many charming talents. She could switch up in a heartbeat and charm any ethnicity, business individual or whoever, and it worked every time.

"Now are you sure you don't need medical attention? That cut looks sorta deep and you might need stitches," he stated.

"No, I'll be fine, but thanks for your concern," she flirted, looking into his eyes.

That's when he noticed her sex appeal. Nestaja stood 5'7" with light brown eyes that complemented her light complexion. She weighed about 175. She was thick and curvy with size 38C breasts and a nice firm-shaped booty. He could tell by her hands, hair, and feet that she kept herself well-maintained. Focusing on her demeanor, he could also tell she was hood. He somewhat lost focus on his job until he saw that her hands were bleeding. "What happened to your hands?" he questioned.

"I smashed them in the car door," she answered. "Both of them?" he asked with surprise.

"Yes, I was moving a little too fast and got a little clumsy." She giggled.

He gave her a look of disbelief and continued writing on his little notepad. Nestaja looked towards her house and noticed two officers entering.

"Why are they going inside my house?" she asked.

"We need to check for weapons, since both callers stated there were some involved."

Nestaja remained calm and prayed that Asia had stashed the guns in a good place. Once the officers entered into the house, they asked that everyone inside come out. Once Asia and the children came out on the front porch, the rest of the officers went in to begin their search. The look on Asia's face didn't sit too well with Nestaja. She could tell something was wrong, but didn't want the officers to become suspicious, so she walked over to comfort Josiah and Jasmine, assuring them everything would be okay. Jasmine didn't like the fact that her daddy was in handcuffs sitting on the curb next to Craz. That wasn't a good sight for a child to see. She began to ask questions.

"Mommy, is my daddy going to jail for beating you up in the room?" "No, Jasmine, we weren't fighting, we were just talking loud."

"But I heard him say 'God, please don't let this bad word be dead', and that's when me and Josiah started knocking on your door."

"No, baby girl, he was talking on the phone to one of his friends about his dog."

"Well, Mommy, what are all those red marks on your neck, and why are you talking like a white lady?"

After noticing Officer Waters was looking her way and taking notes, Nestaja ignored Jasmine's question. "Go sit on the porch with your brother, sweetie. Mommy needs to see what's going on." Nestaja became a little paranoid since the other officers hadn't come out and she could hear them rummaging through her things.

"What's going on in there, Officer Waters?" she asked.

"My team has to do a thorough investigation. Once they're done, you'll be free to go back inside."

"Well, I need to go in now. This is my house, and I want to see what's going on." "Sorry, Ms. Simmons, but I can't let you go in."

"Well, I feel like I'm being violated, since all of the people involved are outside. What the hell they need to be in my house searching for? Tell them if they think anybody has anything, they need to come search out here and not in my house. I already told you ain't nothing in there," she said in an angry tone, starting to let her true colors show.

"Well, what is this?" one officer interrupted as he walked out of the house holding a pencil with a .9 MM dangling from it.

"It's whatever you think it is," Nestaja sarcastically replied.

"Oh, don't get smart, ma'am. This weapon was found in your daughter's room in a bag with some men's clothing along with four bottles of promethazine - or should I say lean. We have so many charges we can file against you, you might want to shut the fuck up and do what we say."

"Don't tell me to shut up. You need to put that gun and lean you claim you found back in your pocket cuz you ain't found shit in my house."

Nestaja looked over at the squad car with Reggie in the back watching while another officer was taking the cuffs off of Craz.

"Ms. Simmons! You care to explain? You know this is considered child endangerment and we can take your kids away from you."

"What? Y'all ain't taking my kids from me. I ain't neva seen that gun!" Nestaja knew that it was Asia's gun and that she must have dropped it in Reggie's bag that she had previously packed and put in Jasmine's room, hoping he would get the picture that she didn't want him there anymore or sleeping in her room. So she started moving his things to his daughter's room, since he claimed she was the reason he was still there. But of course, she wasn't going to say anything.

"Well, Ms. Simmons, looks like you're going to take a ride with us," the officer stated. "No, the fuck I'm not!" she screamed in a raging tone. "And y'all will be hearing from

my lawyer, puttin' shit in my house, tryna set a bitch up and take my kids. Fuck y'all muthafuckas!" she said while eyeing the white Buick lacrosse with dark tinted windows approaching her house.

Officer Waters headed over to the vehicle and they begin talking in a very low tone. A few seconds later, a homely Caucasian woman got out and headed her way. As they approached her, Officer Waters introduced the mystery lady.

"Ms. Simmons, this is Mrs. Mosley. She's a social worker, and she will be taking your kids for a few days until we can figure out if you're fit to keep them in your custody."

"What the fuck you mean?" Nestaja yelled.

"Lower your voice and calm down now!" another officer screamed.

"Cuz, fuck you! You tellin' me you takin' my kids away and you want me to remain calmed down? Y'all got me fucked up."

"Well, if you would pick and choose your boyfriends and friends wisely, you wouldn't have these types of issues," the officer standing next to her chimed in.

Nestaja's mind suddenly went blank and everything went silent. All she could hear were her children crying and begging. "Mommy, please don't let them take us!"

But this was completely out of her control, and she knew her kids depended on her for everything and she always came through. But this time, she had no clue what was she going to do. Despite the hood life she lived, she was actually a really good mother. She never exposed her kids to her hood life. They both were straight-A students. Josiah was known for playing football and doing extra work on popular movie sets, and Jasmine was a cheerleader, played the violin, and was active in gymnastics. They both attended private schools and were some very respectable children.

With all this in mind and seeing them fighting, crying, and begging not to go, Nestaja lost it, charging at the officer closest to her, taking her frustrations out on his face - boom, boom, fist to jaw, fist to eye. She was immediately rushed by the other officers and placed in a chokehold and cuffed. Nestaja was known for her unique hand skills when it came to fighting. She didn't care who or where if she felt disrespected. She would take off on anybody. The only person she really couldn't do much to was Reggie. It wasn't that she was afraid of him. It was more the feelings she held deep inside toward him. Despite all the cheating, lying, abuse, disrespect, and embarrassment he brought her way, she still cared for him and didn't want to cause him any harm.

Ghetto Diva

As she was placed in the police car, Craz yelled out, "Baby, I'm coming to get you out in a few hours. Don't trip; I got you."

She looked over at Asia and couldn't bear the sad look her sister had on her face. Her big puppy dog eyes were full of tears. Nestaja could tell that Asia wanted so badly to take the blame for her sisters arrest but couldn't, due to the fact that she had been on the run for the past few years for a murder. She had a new identity but knew if her prints were run, there was a chance the felony warrant would come up. Nestaja wasn't tripping because that was her baby sister and she knew her situation could cause Asia to be put away for life, as opposed to Nestaja going and bailing out to fight the case on the street with a lawyer.

She gave her sister that "don't worry, it's going to be all right" look and hollered out the window, "Go over Akira's house so I can call and lock up my house. I'll be out in a few hours."

Chapter 2

Riiiing, Riiiing!

"Hello?" Akira answered.

"This is the operator with a collect call from - Nestaja! *Will you accept the charges?"*

"Yes!"

"What's up, Akira?" Nestaja happily asked through the phone receiver.

"That sorry-ass baby daddy of yours is what's up! He betta be glad I wasn't there, or his ass woulda been leaving with the coroner's instead of the police."

"Akira, you crazy!" Nestaja replied, knowing Akira hated Reggie, so she tried to avoid the conversation.

"Bitch, I'm serious! He only doin' that shit cuz you won't let the homies get his ass. Fuck him, Nestaja. He don't give a fuck about you or them kids. If he did, he wouldn't be doing this shit. Y'all ain't even together. That nigga need to get hands put on him. Owwww, I wish I was there! I woulda molly-whopped his ass myself!"

"Akira, we can chop it up about all that when I get out of this hell hole." "Who's comin' to get you?" Akira asked.

"Craz should be on his way!"

"Now that's who got my respect. Nestaja, that nigga love yo' ass. I heard he came through like the bone crusher, but your silly ass stopped him. You shoulda let him handle his business."

"We'll get into all that later. Where's Asia?"

"She went to the store with Crystal to get some blunts," Akira answered.

"Call Craz and link him in on the call. I need to know if he's on his way to get me up outta here before these warrants come up."

"What they charge you with?" Akira asked.

"Assault on an officer, possession of a firearm, and child endangerment."

"Damn, bitch, with them kinda charges, it ain't gon' matter if some punk-ass traffic warrants come up!"

"Akira, just call Craz. I need to get up outta here."

"I don't need to call him. He outside blowin' the horn. We'll be there in a minute." "Hurry up. I don't like bein' in this raggedy-ass place wit' these ratchet-ass broads." "Yeah, whatever, Nestaja. Just keep ya legs closed and they won't try to get between 'em."

"Akira, shut up and get here!" Nestaja replied with an attitude. "Oh, my bad, you might like that, huh?" Akira stated.

"Bye, Akira!" Nestaja angrily yelled into the receiver, disconnecting the call with an attitude.

It wasn't out of the ordinary for them to talk to each other like this. They were all like sisters. Akira had been in Asia's and Nestaja's lives since they were in elementary school. They grew up on the same block, a few doors down from each other, more like family than friends.

Akira was the one out of the bunch that was always getting tested by others because of her innocent bougie looks, but she was a true rider. Those that put her to the test would get fooled by her quick left and her overwhelming strength. Since her mom was Japanese and her dad was Jamaican, she was blessed with an exotic look. Akira stood 5'5", weighing 150 pounds with a nice curvy frame, light caramel complexion, and long, jet-black silky hair.

Whenever the girls would get into an altercation with other females, they would always call her out to fight because she had the looks of a rich saditty girl, nothing like the hood diva she was. To their surprise, she was the roughest one in the pack. She was like a pitbull in a rage. She was very feminine, but when it came to fighting, she was the one that would take off first and beat up a few, with or without help, no matter how many there were.

"Hey ma, what's your name?" a tall chocolate girl asked Nestaja. "Nestaja. Why, you think you know me or something?"

"No, but I would like to know you," she said, moving in closer.

In Nestaja's mind, she wanted to take off on the girl, but something was keeping her from doing so. "Naw, I don't get down that way," Nestaja sternly replied.

"You haven't stumbled across the right female, because I know I can make you feel better than any man has ever made you feel."

Now this bitch is testing me, and I'ma have to beat her ass if she get at me like this again, Nestaja thought. "I doubt that, cuz dick do me good, dick do me right. If I want to taste pussy, I'll suck my juices off my nigga's dick after I get off of it," Nestaja said with much attitude.

"Oh, you a lil freak," the chocolate girl commented.

"Yep, when it comes to sex with my man," Nestaja emphasized.

"Okay ma, I get the picture, you strictly dickly. But you seem like a cool female. What you in here for?" the chocolate girl asked.

"Some bullshit!" Nestaja answered.

"We're all in here for some bullshit. What they charge you with?" "Assault on an officer, possession of a weapon, and child endangerment."

"These suckas always tryna twist you some kinda way. But don't trip, my mom is a good lawyer. Her name is Stacy Johnson. Here is my number, gimme a call. I'ma tell her what's up with you. I'm more than sure she will represent you, since you're a friend of mine."

"Stacy Johnson is your mother? I heard of her, she's good. Thank you for the info, I'm definitely going to get at you. What's your name?" Nestaja asked.

"My name is Tajaye, but everybody calls me Taj."

"Okay Taj, I'm going to hit you up because I'm going to need a good lawyer to get these haters off my back, and your mom's got a good reputation. I know you don't have to worry about nothing, having her as your mother. What are you in here for anyway?" Nestaja asked.

"I'm here for some bullshit too, girl, assault on my ex-mother-in-law. She took my kids and I went to get them back, and one thing led to another and here I am. My brother is on his way to come get me now."

"Oh, that's what's up. My folks should be here in a minute too. I hate this place. It's dirty and these females smell like DWP disconnected their water months ago. "

"Man, you don't have to tell me!" Taj replied with a laugh. "What area you live in?" Nestaja asked

"I just got a place in Ladera for me and my kids. I left my husband's sorry ass. He couldn't decide if he wanted to be with me or his new project Kenneth, so I'm cool."

"You and your husband are both bisexual?" Nestaja asked in surprise.

"Yes, and it was creating a problem in our marriage. I did it to please him, although I did like it. I never let it interfere with our marriage. He stopped spending time with us, started staying the night with his lover, going on trips. It had got to the point where I would only see my husband on payday when it was time for him to give me child support and pay the bills.

I couldn't take it no more, so I packed our things and left. Now he wants to go to counseling and make it work. He scarred me bad. I don't want anything to do with a man. A woman will understand my needs and wants. A man will probably just reopen the wound," Taj sadly stated.

"You don't know what you're missing, girl, 'cause me and my dude go hard. We have no sexual hang-ups, he gives it to me good, when and wherever I want it," Nestaja bragged.

"Daayaam! Sounds like you and him got the sex game on lock," Taj responded. "Yes, girl, and we good at what we do!" Nestaja added.

"Well, my husband wasn't all that great. His package was short and he didn't know how to work it," Taj replied.

"How long were y'all together?" "Fifteen years!"

"FIFTEEN YEARS! Damn, girl, you've been deprived! You betta leave those females and plastic toys alone and get you some real dick. You'd be surprised at how good it can do you, 'cause my nigga keep my poon-poon squirtin' all over the place," Nestaja said, going into deep thought about how good Craz made her feel.

"ATTENTION, INMATES! I'M GOING TO CALL A LIST OF NAMES. IF YOU HEAR YOURS, PLEASE FORM A SINGLE FILE LINE AT THE BLUE DOOR TO YOUR RIGHT SO YOU CAN BE RELEASED."

"Damn, I hope they call me. I'm ready to get up outta this place," Taj stated. "TYWANA JACOBS, ROBIN SILBERBLATT, TAJAYE JOHNSON, ERIKA GOMEZ, CONNIE DURAN, NESTAJA SIMMONS, GEORGETTA LOPEZ, SAMANTHA ESTRELLA, AND JUANNA CHAVEZ. PLEASE COME TO THE DOOR TO YOUR RIGHT SO YOU CAN BE RELEASED."

"Thank God, we outta here," Taj said as they walked out of the holding cell. "Nestaja, call me so we can talk sometime. I know you're not down with the get down, so I promise not to get at you like that anymore. I can tell you're a good friend, and Lord knows I need one."

"Okay, Taj, I'm gonna call you tomorrow so I can hook up with your mom. Here, take my number too. Call me anytime you wanna talk."

"Thanks, Nestaja, I will."

"Okay, talk to you soon." They embraced each other and went their separate ways. "Who was that?" Akira sarcastically asked.

"Damn, Akira, why?"

"I knew you couldn't keep your legs closed, not even for a female. I knew you went that way."

"Akira, you need to shut the fuck up sometime. You don't know what you're talking about."

"Yes I do. That girl is gay. She be on the west side trying to mess with every female over there, and I seen her at a few clubs in Hollywood."

"What you know about these clubs and west side spots?"

"You'd be surprised at what I do when I'm not in the hood. But this ain't about me; it's about your friend. It's obvious, Nestaja. She wants what you got. She don't like dick. She likes you," Akira joked.

"Fuck you, Akira! Where's Craz?" "He went to the bathroom."

"He needs to hurry up, cuz I'm ready to get the hell outta here."

"Bitch, you know Reggie's scandalous ass had his folks that work for Child Services release the kids to his momma."

"Are you serious? How do you know?"

"We tried to go get them, but they said the children were released to the father's mother,"

Akira answered.

"This muthafucka!" Nestaja angrily yelled.

"Hey babe, you okay?" Craz asked, walking up to embrace her. "I will be as soon as I get my kids. Is Reggie still locked up?"

"Yeah, he got a parole hold on him," Akira responded.

"I need to get my kids," Nestaja said as they got into Craz's truck. "Well, what you wanna do?" Akira asked.

"I don't know. Let me think on it."

"Well, bitch, you know I got you. Whatever you decide, I'm wit' it," Akira stated. "Okay, but we have to be careful, because any wrong move can cause me to lose my

rights and my freedom. So give me a minute to think about it. Baby, can you drop me off to my car? I'm goin' over to Akira's house for a few hours and I'll meet you back at my house later. I need to put something together."

"Nestaja, I'm not about to let you go do nothing by yourself."

Nestaja stopped him in mid-sentence. "I'm not! I'm takin' Asia and Akira with me." "NO, NESTAJA!" Craz demanded.

She cut him off again. "I got this, Craz! Baby, trust me," Nestaja said as she looked in his eyes, reaching over and gently massaging his manhood. "I'll meet you at the house tonight and I'll have something special for you," she said in a seductive tone.

Craz wasn't a softy. He was a known killa on the streets and well-respected with lots of money and power. But Nestaja knew his weak points, and when she needed to, she would rub him right to get what she wanted. She knew she was his weakness, and she would sometime use it to her advantage. She had a way with him like no other woman had ever had. She cared for him a great deal, but not as much as he cared for her.

Truth be told, she was still in love with S Man, her teenage sweetheart that she had before Craz and Reggie. He had gotten arrested years ago and had to do a significant amount of time. He didn't want her to put her life on hold, so he told her to do her thing, just look out for him from time to time, and not to get caught up with sucka-ass niggas, because he wanted to build something with her when he got out. She stood by his side in spite of what they went through.

She never let anyone tear down the love they built. Because of that and the history they shared, when he got convicted, she was on point with writing, sporadic visits, and making sure he was comfortable during the time he had to be there.

So Craz was just really someone she met to pass the time, fill in the financial gaps, and provide sexual services as needed. Because of his gangster demeanor, she caught feelings for him. He didn't have a clue that she was going to be with S Man when he came home, but everybody else did. He was her first, and they spent a lot of time together as teenagers. He was from a gang on the west side, and she was an east side chick. They met when Nestaja's parents separated and her dad moved to the west side. He was a few years older than she was and he had a lot of street game, so she looked up to him, she admired him, she analyzed each and every word he spoke to her, she valued his opinion, and most importantly, he taught her all the game he knew. He was the one that molded her into the hustling woman that she was today.

Nestaja would go spend weekends and summer vacations at her dad's house so she could spend time with S Man. Years passed, and S Man and Nestaja were still together, but having many problems as teens. He cheated on her a few times, had a few babies. Even though Nestaja was deeply hurt, she hung in there because she knew that S Man was her soulmate. He was doing his dirt, but they never broke up. They ended up moving together, and he made sure she was well taken care of and didn't have to lift a finger to do anything. Although he was young and trying different things, his actions showed where his heart truly was.

A while back, S Man went out of state to get his money right and Nestaja slowly faded out of the picture. When he came back to L.A. a year later, to his surprise, she had a huge belly that was about to pop any day. He was truly hurt, but he had to man up and do his thing to get over her. But deep down inside, they both knew they would find their way back to each other.

Craz, on the other hand, was cool, but he had a lot of bitches that he thought Nestaja didn't know about. He took damn good care of her and her kids, and would put his life and freedom on the line for them. He would also do the same thing for the rest of his females.

Because of this, she couldn't bring herself to fall completely in love with him. She also cared for Reggie a lot, had a baby by him, and was in a long-term relationship with him. Even he knew that her heart was really with S Man.

After a few ear nibbles and kisses on the neck, Craz agreed to meet Nestaja at her house at 11:30 that night. He took her to her car so she and Akira could go to her house, meet up with the girls, and figure out what their next move was going to be.

Chapter 3

In the car on the way to Akira's house, the two girls rolled in silence. Nestaja was in deep thought about what she was going to do to get her kids, and Akira was thinking about how she was going to put some extra money in her pocket. The usual five minute drive down Avalon seemed like an hour. When they finally arrived, they noticed a big black truck parked in Akira's driveway like it belonged there.

"Who is that?" Akira asked.

"This is your house. How am I supposed to know?" Nestaja responded. "You got your heat on you?" Akira asked.

"Yeah, you know where the stash is."

Akira disassembled the side door and pulled out a 40 Glock. The girls got out of the car and creeped up on the truck. As they got closer, they could see there was a male on the driver's side with his head leaned back on the seat like he was asleep. He had to be out of it, they figured, because he never noticed they had driven up. Nestaja grabbed a bat that was lying nearby and she tiptoed to the passenger side while Akira walked up closer with the Glock cocked and ready to pop. As they got closer, they could see that the driver appeared to be a big guy with a lot of jewelry, but he still wasn't familiar to either of them. As they moved in a little closer, to their surprise, there was Katrina with her face planted in the driver's lap, giving him a sloppy blow job while he leaned back with his eyes closed, enjoying her services.

"Aww, you hoe!" Akira said as she released the bullet out of the chamber.

But Katrina didn't care; she kept doing what she did best, and the driver never moved out of his enjoyable position. The girls were used to Katrina and her lewd acts, so it was nothing. When it came to money, she would do anything and anybody, and it was never for a small fee.

Ghetto Diva

Akira and Nestaja proceeded inside to come up with a plan. Once they got in, Nestaja immediately headed for the bathroom to take a shower because she felt dirty, plus she had to hook up with Craz later. After she showered and freshened up, she threw on a cute and comfortable workout 'fit and matching tennis shoes that she pulled out of her hoe bag, as she called it, that she kept in the trunk of her car. When she finally came out of the bathroom, the whole crew was there: Asia, Crystal, and Katrina. Akira was in the kitchen hooking up one of her many specialties - some chicken burritos, refried beans, and Spanish rice with some Kool Aid. The girls sat down and began to put some plans together.

"So what's up, y'all? I need to get my kids back without making a scene."

"Fuck that! I say let's go over there and lay the whole house down and get my niece and nephew," Asia demanded.

"Damn, Asia, you tryna catch us all a case! We gotta do this right so it won't backfire. What I need to do is set the house up some kind of way. I need to make it look like an unsafe place for kids. I gotta move something from one place to another. I know Reggie has a lot of work over there. I just need to locate it and move it to a different spot."

"Nestaja, what you need to do is grab it and make you a few quick dollars. I know somebody that'll buy it all, right now."

"I'll see what's up with that later," Nestaja replied.

"If you want to set him up, I got a cool police friend that's with the business. I ran into him when me and Craz came to bail you out. He tryna fuck wit'cha girl and will do anythang for me."

"Well, Akira, you need to find out what's up with him. We can use him for a lot of stuff." "Fuck that nigga! I don't like no police, and I don't trust 'em," Asia added.

"I don't like Reggie's bitch ass," Katrina blurted out.

"It's cool. I'm going to go to his mother's house in Inglewood and check my traps. I gotta see what's over there and what I'm up against," Nestaja decided.

"Enough about Reggie. I got a cool lick for us," Katrina danced around, bragging. "That nigga I was outside with in the truck – he left twenty stacks and some work in the room, and he ain't goin' back until later. He was on his way to Victorville when he left here. He don't like rollin' with money on him. He left it all in that room. His wife put him out last week, and he ain't got nowhere else to put it. The good thing is, I'm not the only one that knows where he been restin' his head, because some lil dust bucket broad came to the door for him while we were kicking it, and another one called and asked him did she leave her ring there. But I already got that," Katrina said as she flashed a three-carat diamond ring.

"Well, what the hell are we waiting for?" Crystal chimed in. "Damn, Katrina, you always got a good lick," Asia added.

"Bitch, what you thought? I don't suck dick and fuck for free. When I do my dirt, trust me, it's gonna always be beneficial. Even though I can't stand my baby daddy DJ, I'm going to always respect the fact that the punk takes care of me and my kids. So I'm going to make sure when I do my dirt outside of home, I'm going to always bring something back to the table. Y'all with it or no?" Katrina asked.

"I'm not. Y'all go on. I'm going to Inglewood right quick to see my kids. I know they're worried," Nestaja responded.

"I'm goin' wit'cha," Crystal added.

"Naw, I'm good. Me and his momma is cool. As long as Reggie ain't there, I'm straight.

I'ma go see what I'm up against and ease my kids' minds. I know they're scared and wanna know what's up with me. I'll see y'all in the morning. I'm sure you bitches will be wide awake and ready to shop after the come-up. Once I see the kids and get some rest, I'll be able to think with a clear head, because right now, I don't know if I'm coming or going," Nestaja explained.

"Well, if you need us, call us. We're always on standby," Crystal added.

"Alright, y'all, be careful, and call me when it's over and done with so I'll know y'all good."

Nestaja headed out to her car. Before she drove off, her cell phone began to ring. *I know it ain't Craz because it's only 9:00 p.m. I just left the girls, so who could it be?* she thought. She grabbed the phone out of her purse and was surprised that Reggie's momma's number was on the caller ID. "Hello?" she answered.

"Nestaja, this Tasha. The kids been crying for you, and I thought I'd call to see if you got out."

"Where are they?" Nestaja asked. "In the back room watchin' TV."

"I'm on my way over there now. Did they eat yet?" "No, not yet."

"Okay, I'm going to grab them their favorite and I'll be there in a few."

Nestaja started up her car. As she drove off, she began to cry. She was a good mother to her kids. She provided for them the best way she could. When life threw her lemons, she made lemon meringue pie, lemonade, and lemon chicken. She was a hustler at heart. No matter what the situation was, her kids knew Mommy would come through with a plan that would work. She couldn't let them down. She was willing to do anything to get her kids back.

She got their food and headed to Inglewood. When she got there, there was a lot of commotion going on in the front of the house. There were also a lot of girls there that didn't look familiar to her. She parked her car, got out, and headed inside, but her kids weren't anywhere to be found. She went back outside and spotted Reggie's sister Tasha in the crowd and approached her.

To Nestaja's surprise, four of the girls rushed her. She didn't get her burner back from Akira because she didn't think she'd need it. These girls were pretty big, and she was definitely outnumbered. She picked one out of the bunch and went head up with her while the others served her with punches from every angle. This fight wasn't in her favor, but she was determined to hurt at least one of them. She fought until she saw blood. She thought it belonged to the girl that she was focused on, but it wasn't. It was her own.

That didn't stop her. She kept fighting, even though she wasn't anywhere near winning.

One of the girls tripped and a blade fell from her pocket. Nestaja gained some strength and grabbed it, but as she went to reach for the blade, she felt a sharp object pierce her thigh. She still managed to get it, and she begun to swing like she was in a tennis match. It became obvious to her that she touched a few of them, because they started to back up off of her. Tasha didn't expect it to go as far as it did. She was just doing what her brother asked her to do.

When it was over, there was blood everywhere, and Tasha became nervous, not knowing what to do. She knew she had again let her brother talk her into doing his dirty work, and she would be the one to suffer the consequences.

Nestaja made her way to her car and drove herself to the hospital. Once she got out, she stood there for a second. As she made an attempt to go inside, she fainted. Luckily, a gentleman saw her and called for help.

Chapter 4

"Nestaja! This is my fourth time leaving a message. It's 11:47 and I been sittin' outside your house since 11:03. If you wasn't fucking with me, you shoulda said that. I don't know

what's up wit' you, but shit ain't been right lately. I can't put my finger on it, but you got me fucked up if you think I'ma let you play me like this. You do you, and I'ma do me. I'm cool on you, bitch. Goodbye!"

This bitch got a gangsta fucked up! Craz thought as he drove off from Nestaja's house.

I put my life and my freedom on the line fuckin' with this bitch and her baby daddy, and this is what I get in return. I give her and her kids the world. She knows anything she needs or wants I got her. But fuck that, I don't need her. She needs me, if anything, and I'ma show her ass how cool I am on her. Shit, I'm gangsta, fuck her!

Craz thoughts were interrupted by his cell phone ringing. "What's up?" he answered. "Craz, this is Asia. Tell Nestaja to answer her phone."

"She not wit' me, sis, I thought she was still wit' y'all."

"Nah, she left us about 9:00 on her way to Reggie's momma's house to see the kids." "And y'all ain't talked to her since?

"No, we thought she was with you. We been calling her phone for the last hour.

Something ain't right. I'm going to Reggie's momma's house to see if she still there with the kids."

"Okay, sis, let me know what's up."

***

The girls were en route to Akira's house to get dressed to go to the club after they came up on the lick Katrina had turned them on to.

"Akira, we need to make a detour to Reggie's momma's house," Asia said in an angry tone.

"Why, what's up?" Akira asked.

"I don't know, but Nestaja ain't with Craz and she ain't answering her phone. Something ain't right."

Akira busted a U-turn in the middle of Western and pushed up Imperial on their way to Inglewood. She put her V-6 to use. She violated about ten traffic laws, turning the usual fifteen minute trip into nine minutes. When they arrived, the house was dark like no one was there, no cars in the yard or anything. Asia thought she'd get out and knock on the door, thinking they might be in the back asleep or something. She knocked and knocked, but didn't get an answer.

Akira parked her car near a bush in the front of the house so they could get out and pee. As Asia walked back to the car, she noticed something shining on the ground. As she got closer, she noticed it was Nestaja's charm from her chain. She knew it was her sister's because not too many people had a diamond-studded 7 with a crown on it. When she went to pick it up, she noticed blood all over the ground. She became very agitated, not knowing what was going on.

"Hey Asia, look at this!" Crystal said while pulling her pants up from peeing. "Is this Nestaja's chain?"

"Yeah, and this is the charm to it," Asia added. "What's all this blood on the ground?" Katrina asked.

"I don't know, but we damn sure about to find out. Where is the closest hospital?" Asia questioned.

"I don't know, I think it's Kaiser," Crystal answered. "Nah, Cris, its Centinela," Katrina assured her.

They jumped back in the car and rushed off to the hospital. When they arrived, Asia and Crystal went in while Akira and Katrina looked for a place to park.

"Excuse me, Miss, I would like to know if you have a patient by the name of Nestaja Simmons."

Ghetto Diva

"Can you fill out the form and return it to me?" a dark-skinned girl wearing a blonde synthetic wig and cheap pink lipstick replied with an attitude while she chewed her gum, holding the phone up to her ear with her shoulder.

"Miss, this is an emergency! I just want to know if my sister is here. Can you just look on your computer, please?"

"Look, this is a hospital. Everyone in here is an emergency. When you fill out this form and bring it back, if I have the time, I'll look," the receptionist answered as she rolled her eyes, swirling her chair around with her back to Asia so she could continue with her phone conversation.

"Look, lady, I don't want any problems," Asia said while Crystal filled out the form. "I'm just looking for my sister."

"Well, I'm about to go to lunch, but I can probably do it when I get back."

Asia and Crystal snapped. Akira and Katrina walked in and noticed all the commotion going on. They immediately jumped into their defensive mode.

"What's crackin'?" Akira asked.

"Oh, who are they, y'all lil bodyguards or something?" The receptionist giggled. Akira leaped over the counter and attacked her. Katrina leaped over to get Akira. *"LADIES, BREAK IT UP NOW!"* a stern voice demanded.

As Akira released the receptionist, to her surprise, there stood her officer friend. "Would you four come with me please?" the officer commanded.

The girls walked off with the officer. Asia was looking around, planning her escape, not knowing the officer was a good friend of Akira's. She had a look on her face that told the other girls to find out what was up with Nestaja, because she was out. Akira shook her head no in such a way that Asia somewhat felt that Akira was telling her it was okay. But Asia hated the police and didn't trust any of them.

As they waited for the elevator, the officer began to talk to Akira. "What's up with you, sexy? We bumped into each other twice in one day. That means it's heaven sent," he said in a happy kinda way.

"Officer Waters, you're not trying to mess with a hood female like me."

"You can call me Kenneth," Officer Waters said in a flirty tone. "And yes, I am interested, sexy. I'm digging your style, baby. When can I take you out?" he asked.

"We can hook something up later."

Asia took a good look at the officer. That's when she realized he was the same one that had come to Nestaja's house earlier that day. *Hmmm, he on the homegirl. He can be our exit up outta all this bullshit we got in today*, Asia thought. "Excuse me, can you find out if my sister is here?" Asia asked.

"Sure, what is her name?" "Nestaja Simmons!"

"That name sounds really familiar," he said as he looked at Asia as if he had seen her before. "Excuse me, but I had a really hectic day, I can't remember my own damn name sometimes. But I'll check right now. Don't worry about the little altercation downstairs. I'll take care of it," he said as they stepped off the elevator. He walked over to a computer and asked Asia, "How do you spell the first name?"

"N-E-S-T-A-J-A Simmons."

"Okay, yes, she is here, but she is in surgery right now." "For what?" Asia asked in a frantic tone.

"I'm not too sure. Give me a minute and I'll find out. I'll be right back."

As he walked away, the girls became very quiet. They were all in deep thought, thinking about what could have happened. Was she going to be okay, and how serious was it? Asia called Craz to let him know what was going on, and he told her he was on his way.

Feeling somewhat guilty because he thought she was playing him. Craz jumped in his big fast truck and headed to the hospital to be by Nestaja's side. When he arrived, the girls were talking to the officer, and he could tell that he was giving them some type of information because Katrina had out her tablet, asking questions and putting information in it. When the officer walked away, Craz walked over to see what was going on.

Asia was very hurt and upset. When he walked over to her, she immediately buried her head into his chest and cried. Asia and Craz had a real brother/sister relationship. It was him that bailed her out of jail when she caught her case. He got her a new identity and told her what she needed to do to say free.

Crystal began to explain. "Some bitches that work for Reggie jumped Nestaja at Reggie's momma's house. His sister set it all up. Nestaja got stabbed in the back and the upper thigh. The blade broke in her thigh and they had to remove it. She lost a lot of blood, so they had to give her a blood transfusion. She just came out of surgery. We'll be able to go in and talk to her within the next half hour."

Craz's blood began to boil. He became mad at himself for letting her go without him. He grew even angrier because it was Reggie's doing. He felt he should had taken care of him when the opportunity presented itself. *If only I would have told her no, this would have never happened,* he thought. "Do y'all know who jumped her?" he asked.

"Well, the officer said a neighbor by the name of Mrs. Fulbright made a call and told him everything, and a Tasha Salazar was arrested shortly after the incident occurred," Crystal answered.

"Who is Tasha?" he asked. "Reggie's sister," Crystal answered.

"So what are we going to do?" Katrina stood up asking. "This nigga got us fucked up, for real! Nestaja be on that nice shit, talkin' about, 'this my baby daddy, don't do nothing to him, I got it.' Yeah, look where it got her. I know he put his sister up to this, cuz she ain't that type. She's an older lady that's about forty-seven with three sets of twins, and her husband started smoking and ended up leaving her and the kids so he can chase crack."

"How do you know all this, Katrina?" Craz asked.

"We was all cool when Nestaja and Reggie first got together. I used to do her and her friends' hair. It was when he started putting hands on Nestaja and getting disrespectful when we stopped fucking with him and his family. We just need to find out who each and every one of them bitches are, because they all have to pay for this. I'm taking this to the hood. Nestaja might be mad at me, but she'll get over it. It's all out of love," Katrina said as she paced the floor with her fists balled up.

"Don't trip. We're going to take care of this as soon as we get all the information," Craz commented.

"You know Nestaja gon' be on one when she gets better. So, I'm sure she is going to put them baby daddy feelings to the side and do what's right," Crystal added.

"Will the family for Nee-stay…Nee-stay-jah Simmons please come to the reception counter?"

Akira abruptly ended her conversation with Kenneth and headed over to the reception counter while the others got up and hurried over to the area as well.

"We're the family for Nestaja Simmons."

"Hello, I'm Doctor Cushner and I performed the surgery on Ms. Simmons. We were able to remove the blade that broke off in her quadrate muscle and she is doing just fine. Everything went well."

"What the hell is a quadrate muscle?" Asia asked.

"That's the muscle in her upper thigh," Dr. Cushner answered. "Ms. Simmons is in recovery, waiting to see some familiar faces, I'm sure. She is in room 467. I'll walk you over. Now let me inform you, she is still a little sedated, so she may dose off a little and not be aware of her surroundings. But once the medicine wears off, she will be back to her normal self."

"Okay, thank you, Doctor Cushner," Asia thanked him.

"You're more than welcome, and here is my card just in case you have any questions." "Okay, and thanks again."

"Asia, stop flirting with Doctor Cushner," Crystal added to lighten the situation.

Everyone burst into laughter, which caused Nestaja to wake up. "Hey Momma, I'll be ready to go in a minute, just let me get some rest. I took the kids to the amusement park and I'm tired," Nestaja said in a slurred tone.

"Yeah, this bitch is fucked up like she had some kinda bomb antidote," Katrina joked. "The anesthesia hasn't worn off yet, so bear with her a little," the doctor informed them. "Asia, did you call your mother?" Craz asked.

"No, not yet. She's still on her spiritual tour. I don't want her to lose focus. Everything looks fine, so we can call her when Nestaja gets outta here."

"You need to call her now so she can pray while she is on her spiritual crusade tour," Crystal stated.

"I'll call her when we leave here. I just don't feel like hearing her fuss about us not bein' in church like she raised us, and that's why all of this is happening to us and so on…"

"Asia, y'all blessed to have a mother that is an evangelist that speaks all over the world," Crystal stated.

"I'm going to call her a little later. If I call now, she's gonna wanna talk to Nestaja, and this sleepy bitch can't even talk to us and we're right here."

"Nestaja!" Craz called. "Can you hear me, baby?"

"Yeah, I hear you, S Man. I'm so tired, baby. Wake me up when it's time to take the kids to school, sweetie. Love you."

The girls looked at each other in disbelief. Katrina let out a long "ooooowwww". Akira dropped her mouth, and Asia walked away. Of course, Crystal cracked a joke to ease the tension.

"She real high, thinking she Lois Lane on the set with Superman." Everyone chuckled.

"Now that we know she okay, let's let her get some rest so her high can come down and she can tell us what really happened," Crystal suggested.

"Well, Kenneth gave me some information - not much, but he's going to try to get more," Akira responded.

"That's the officer friend of yours you told us about earlier?" Asia asked in a very questioning tone.

"Yeah, why, what's up?"

"That's the asshole that came to Nestaja's house and took her to jail and got the kids taken."

"Oh, is he?" Akira replied. "Yes, he is, Akira."

"Well, that may just make our mission a little easier," Akira said in a conniving tone. "What you mean?" Asia asked.

"Don't trip, but I guarantee Nestaja's charges get dropped and she gets her kids back. I got too much dirt on him, and he'll do any and everything for me. I'm going to use this to my advantage," Akira informed Asia.

"Craz, you straight?" Katrina asked.

"Yeah, I'm good. I'm going to stay the night here with Nestaja. I don't wanna leave my truck here overnight, so can you take it on the block and put it up for me? I'll have one of the homies pick me up tomorrow," Craz said to Katrina.

"Okay, I got you."

Chapter 5

"Reggie Salazar, you have a visitor."

Reggie jumped off his bunk and headed towards the visiting area, not caring who it was. He was just excited to get a visit and tell someone what happened in court. While walking to the visiting area, he ran into his homeboy Ghost.

"Waddup Blood?" Reggie greeted him.

"What's up Jino, my nigga?" Ghost responded, calling Reggie by his street name. "What you in here for?" Ghost asked.

"Fucking with my baby momma."

"Blood, you still with that crazy bitch?"

"Naw, I was over there fuckin' with my kids and the bitch just flipped the script and called the police on a nigga."

"You shoulda touched her up, Blood."

"Oh, I'ma get her when I get out. I already had some of the homegirls put hands on her, but the bitch survived, so I got something for her."

"Ain't she a crab?" Ghost asked.

"Yeah, she from the other side, but what that mean?"

"Well, word on the streets, they been puttin' it down lately. I'm just giving you a heads up. I'm in here on some traffic bullshit. I'll be outta here in a few days. If you need me to do anything, Jino, just let me know, Blood. You know I ain't neva too much cared for your baby momma anyway. I just dealt with her because she was yo' bitch. But fuck her, it's whatever with me," Ghost said.

Now truth be told, Ghost was in love with Nestaja's cousin Katrina. One night, he was chillin' with her at his spot. He sent her to get something to eat in his lowrider and she mysteriously got carjacked.

While that was going on, a nigga and two bitches with ski masks on kicked in his door and took everything he had. They stripped him naked, put a wig and make up on him, took him outside asshole-naked, and tied him to a tree. Luckily, his sister was passing by, saw him tied up, and she freed him. He was too embarrassed to tell anyone.

Since he was sprung on Katrina, he was in denial that she set him up, so he just chalked it up as a loss. But since they took everything from him, he had nothing to keep up with her glamorous lifestyle, so she left him. As the years passed, he was never able to get back on his feet, so he finally accepted the known fact that she set him up. He would see her in traffic pushing all types of expensive cars, shining like a million dollars, and he would be at the bus stop. She even had the nerve to stop one time and offer him a ride. Now that he wasn't in love with her anymore, he was out to get her and anybody that she had any dealings with.

"A'ight, Blood, I'll be out this bitch in a few weeks. I'ma hit you up," Reggie responded.

They gave each other dap and went their separate ways. Reggie sat down with anticipation, waiting to see who was there to visit him.

"Visitor for Salazar, please proceed to the visiting area."

Reggie watched as his mom and the kids walked down the aisle. He was happy to see them and to tell his mom the good news about his case.

Jasmine grabbed the phone first. "Hi, Daddy!"

"Hey, princess! How's Daddy's big girls doing?"

"Fine. Does Mommy go to this school with you?"

"No, Mommy goes to a different school."

"Oh, can we go see her too?"

"No, Mommy's school is real far, and you know your grandmom don't like to drive." "Auntie Asia can take us."

"No, baby! Daddy doesn't know how to call your auntie." "Josiah knows her number, Daddy."

"Well, we'll see when Daddy gets out of school."

"Okay!" Jasmine said as she watched a deputy pace the floor behind her dad. "Daddy, is that your teacher?"

"Yeah, Jasmine, that's one of them."

"Oh, he's watching you while you on recess?" Jasmine asked in a very innocent voice. "Yes, baby!" Reggie responded.

"Oh! Daddy, I want to see Mommy. I don't like it at that stinky lady's house," Jasmine stated.

"What lady?" Reggie asked.

"I don't know. But Grandma said we can't go over her house, so we have to stay at the stinky lady's house."

"Well, it will be okay when Daddy gets out of school." Jasmine began to cry. "I want Mommy!"

Josiah walked over to comfort her. Reggie's mom took the phone. "Hey, what's up, Ma?"

"I don't know, boy. You need to think of something, because these kids need and want their mother. You on some spiteful shit, and I don't want no parts of this, Reggie. Jasmine has been peeing on herself, and I know it's only because of this situation," Ms. Salazar explained.

"Where y'all been stayin'?" Reggie asked.

"We've been over a friend of mine's house that I used to work with. You remember Norma, don't you?"

"On Parmalee Street in Compton?" "Yeah, her!" she replied.

"Yeah, I remember her. Listen, I went to court and they dropped all the charges. I just have to do a 60-day violation, and since the jails are overcrowded, I only have to do 30. I already been in here seven, so I'll be out in about three weeks, but keep that under your hat. I don't want Nestaja's bitch ass to find out."

"Well, Reggie, these kids need their mother." "See, Ma, there you go, taking sides."

"No, Reggie, I'm not taking sides, but it's affecting them in a way you can't even begin to imagine. They don't know if their mother is okay or not. Miss Fulbright called me and told me what happened at the house the other night. You know they came and arrested Tasha for that.

You need to do this the right way, boy. You're affecting other people's lives. Just take her to court, Reggie."

"ATTENTION, VISITORS, YOU HAVE THREE MINUTES REMAINING!"

"A'ight, Momma, we only got three minutes. Let me talk to Josiah, and whatever you do, don't go home. Did you get the $8000 I had stashed?"

"Yeah!"

"Okay, let me holla at Josiah."

"Here, Josiah, Reggie wanna talk to you." "I don't wanna talk right now," Josiah said.

"He don't wanna talk, Reggie."

"Tell that nigga if he don't get on the phone, I'ma whip his lil ass when I come home!" "No, Reggie, I'm not telling him that. He is mad at the situation. He doesn't - "

"ATTENTION VISITORS, YOUR CALLS HAVE BEEN DISCONNECTED AND YOUR VISIT IS OVER."

Ms. Salazar got the kids and headed out of the building, and then the questions began. "Grandma, are we going to ever see Mommy again?" Jasmine asked.

"Yes, Jasmine, you're going to see your mom soon." "Is she okay?"

"Yes, baby, God is going to keep her safe, just like he is going to keep me, you and Josiah safe."

"Well, can God take us to see Mommy?" Ms. Salazar began to cry.

"What's wrong, Grandma?" Jasmine asked.

"Nothing, Jasmine. Grandma has to go to San Diego to pick someone up, but when I come back, I'm going to take you and Josiah to see her," Ms. Salazar responded.

"You promise?" Jasmine asked.

"Yes, baby!" she said as she embraced both Jasmine and Josiah. "You have to pinky promise, Grandma."

"Yes, Jasmine, I pinky promise," she added while locking fingers with Jasmine.

Chapter 6

"Hey, cripple, we're here to pick you up!" Asia shouted as she and Katrina entered the hospital room.

"Good, because I'm ready to get up outta here," Nestaja replied.

"The nurse went to get a wheelchair to wheel your crippled ass to the car," Katrina commented.

"Don't get it twisted. I can maneuver better than you think. Where is Craz?" Nestaja asked.

"I don't know. I called him, but he didn't answer," Asia answered in a suspicious tone. "Did somebody pick my car up, or did y'all leave it here?"

"Damn, Nestaja, why you worried about your car? You got bigger problems than that," Katrina stated.

"So I guess you gon' come chauffeur me around."

"Your car had a lot of blood in it. Craz picked it up and took it to get detailed," Asia added.

"Well, I'm hungry. I wanna go to get something to eat as soon as we leave here." "Umm, don't you think you need to change clothes?" Asia asked, looking at her from

head to toe.

"Change clothes? For what? We can call the order in and go pick it up. And why did you bring me this to put on anyway?"

"This was the only thing I could find at your house for you to wear. Craz didn't get a chance to pick up your clothes from the cleaners," Asia replied.

"Well, let's go to my house first so I can change, then we can go sit down and eat."

"Damn, greedy bitch. You just had surgery a few days ago. Don't you think you should be at home resting?" Katrina commented.

"Didn't I just tell you bitches I'm good? I'm grateful to be alive, and a l lil punk ass surgery don't stop the show. So take me home to change clothes so we can go get something to eat. I want some seasoned food. The stuff they was giving me is worse than the food in the county jail."

"It can't be that bad," Katrina added.

"Let's just go. I been ready to leave since I got here," Nestaja complained while the nurse wheeled her to the car.

Before they could step into Katrina's luxury German car, she immediately stated, "Don't get nothing on my seats! You bitches ain't on your periods, are you? Nurse, you sure them bandages on her ain't leaking."

"Damn, Katrina, you putting a lot on it," Nestaja stated.

"I just got my car detailed. I got ivory interior, and I don't want to mess it up." "I'm sure you'll have cum stains on it before the day is over with."

The girls started laughing at Nestaja's statement because they all knew, knowing Katrina, that she probably would.

"Nestaja! Did you know any of them bitches that jumped you?" Asia asked. "Nope, but we gon' find out, that's fa damn sho'."

"I can't stand your baby daddy! I don't know what you were thinking having a baby by his ass. He ain't even your type."

"Asia, you got to admit, the punk put on a good front when they first met," Katrina added.

"Yeah, Reggie was cool in the beginning. He just got a bit of the freak in me and experienced my housewife qualities, and now he hates that he don't have access like he used to, not to mention my bomb-ass head and pussy."

"You shoulda known that wasn't gon' work. You know what they say: you can't turn a hoe into a housewife," Katrina joked.

"Well, you'll neva get married then!" Nestaja shot back.

Ghetto Diva

As they approached Nestaja's house, she noticed an abnormal amount of cars on her block. But then she thought that the new church on the corner could be having some kind of special service. When Nestaja got out of the car, Craz was right there to greet her with a big hug and kiss. Then he told her to come with him to the back because he wanted to talk to her about something. He helped her walk around to the backyard, and to her surprise, all of her friends and family were there to welcome her home. They had shrimp, lobster, salmon, chicken, and steak on the grill with all the trimmings. *Craz really outdone himself this time,* Nestaja thought as she hugged and thanked him.

"You still want restaurant food?" Katrina giggled.

"Me, Asia, and Craz put all this together at the last minute. Akira and Crystal did all the cooking, and your cousins over there did the decorations and hooked up some mixed drinks and offered to DJ. We just had him turn it down so you wouldn't be suspicious."

"Aww, thank y'all," Nestaja expressed as they embraced in a group hug.

"Come inside and get dressed," Craz said. "I picked up a few things for you today." "Thank you, Craz, you're the best!" she said, anxious to make her way inside to see what he had gotten her.

"Nestaja got a good man," one family member emphasized.

"Girl, yeah, he's beyond ghetto ballin' and takes damn good care of her and them kids," another one replied.

"Umm-hmm! But y'all know he married, right?" their cousin Royal added.

"How you know?" one questioned.

"Girl, his wife works at the post office with my friend Isha, and she seen him at our family Christmas party with Nestaja and told me everything. His wife has another boyfriend, but she still has sex with Craz, and he pays her for it."

"Royal, you stay in everybody else's business but your own. And half the time you don't know what the hell you be talking about," another one added.

"I do though! Isha and his wife was cool until the wife started accusing Isha of messing around with him."

"Well, if that's the case, then why didn't you tell Nestaja?"

"Nestaja knows he ain't shit. She always findin' out something new about his ass. She just keeps it to herself. She was sprung on him until she found out he still messing with a few of his exes on a regular. Nestaja liked him so much she was contemplating leaving S Man. But when she found out what Craz was all about, she decided to play his game with him until it's time for S Man to get out. And I think she be low-key messin' with Reggie too."

"Now there you go, all in Nestaja's mix," one added.

"If I ever get a man like Craz, I would constantly supply him with head, good pussy, cook, clean, and keep pushin' out his kids," Royal boasted.

"Girl, please! Nestaja don't want no kids by him. He got about nine or ten of 'em with like seven or eight baby mamas already. My sis knows what she's doing. She's getting it while the getting is good," Nestaja's oldest sister bragged.

"Yeah, we taught her, Asia, and the rest of them how to break these niggas, cuz they ain't worth shit. They want our goods and we want their money," another cousin added, high-fiving another.

Nestaja looked around and smiled, in awe seeing all of her family. Everyone was there except her parents and a few of her siblings that lived either out of town or far away. She was from a big family. Her mom had become a well-known evangelist after she divorced their dad. She was on a mission for God. She traveled to teach and spread the word. Her dad was the total opposite, a well-known Crip that had retired his blue rag a few years ago. He was just enjoying life at his home in Newport Beach, and he would sometimes get all his grandkids and take them out on his yacht. Both parents were still young. They had gotten married and had their first child when they were 13 and 14.

The backyard boogie was going well - everyone mingling, kids playing, lots of food and drinks. Nestaja was happy that everyone came to welcome her home from the hospital. She was dressed well in an expensive powder-blue and yellow summer dress that hid her recent wounds. They were perfectly matched with a pair of yellow designer sandals - all compliments of Craz. The only thing that was missing were her children. She had gotten really sad when her niece came and asked her why they weren't there. She told her that they were with their dad and would be back soon.

When her doorbell rang, she got up and limped inside to answer it. It was a friend of hers whom she met years ago on a bartending job. They had clicked immediately because they both grew up in the same area. Netra started coming around and ended up being friends with all of the girls. She didn't come over that often because she had a crazy boyfriend that didn't like her being out of his presence. The girls didn't care for him, so her visits were far, few, and brief.

Netra was a project girl. She was just as crazy as her boyfriend. Whatever he would dish out to her, she would give it right back to him - sometimes even worse.

"Hey Netra, what's up wit'cha, girl?"

"I'm cool, girl, but I need to holla at you." "What's up?"

"One of the girls that jumped you lives across the way from me. I was supposed to go with them on that mission. I wish I would have, because I woulda turned on all them hoes when I seen it was you. Oh, and your baby daddy set it all up. He paid them busted-ass bitches forty dollars each and some lines for their noses. They're some real low budget bitches. I didn't know it was Reggie until they came back and was bragging about it. I didn't say nothin'. I just listened. I can help you get all them bitches."

Nestaja was furious at the news Netra had just dropped on her, but she didn't want to let it show because she had plans on playing this game with her baby daddy and getting them all back. She just didn't know who she could trust. "Wow, you just don't know how this made my day," Nestaja responded.

"Hey Netra, what's going on, girl?" Akira walked in, greeting her with a hug. "Netra knows them bitches that jumped me."

"How you know?" Akira asked.

"I was supposed to go with them on that mission, but I didn't go when I found out it was only forty dollars. I didn't know it was Reggie they was dealing with either," Netra stated.

"You still live in the projects?" Nestaja asked.

"No, I been in Leimert Park for a year now," she answered.

"Okay, let's do this then. Come to Akira's house so we can put something together. We will be over there Saturday night at 7:00 p.m."

"I'll be there," Netra replied.

The conversation was interrupted by someone outside blowing a car horn like something was wrong. They looked out the window and could tell it was a female in the car. She was driving a brand new European SUV.

"Who is this bitch?" Katrina questioned. "I don't know!" Crystal answered.

"Me either, but I got my burner on me," Asia added. "I still got yours, Nestaja," Akira added.

"Let's go see who she is," Crystal suggested.

They rushed outside, only to get stopped by Craz. "What y'all doing?"

"Who is that bitch?" Akira shouted.

"Did y'all get a good look?" Craz replied.

Nestaja stepped off the porch and took a good look and realized it was her cousin. "Oh, that's Niko!" she sang.

"She got a new car?" Katrina asked.

"Hey cuzzo!" Niko said as she jumped out of the car.

Niko was another cousin that lived in Calabasas with her husband, who owned a chain of European car dealerships. Craz looked at Niko with a smile and bobbed his head. He was giving her the okay. She tossed the key to Nestaja, saying, "Here, cuz, this is all you."

"Baby, you like it?" Craz asked.

There were screams of happiness from Nestaja. The girls and the rest of the party was now in the front yard admiring the brand new SUV.

"He's buying her all this shit and she don't even like his ass," Royal hated. "That's fucked up! She should tell him that she got anotha nigga. He's going to try to kill her ass when he finds out."

"Damn, Royal, why you gotta hate all the damn time?" one responded.

"Bitch, why do you put the dick and the balls in your mouth at the same time?" another joked.

"Damn, sis, this nigga be looking out for you in a real way. I see he 'bout gettin' his paper too. I need to get back in the game. We need to talk."

"Okay, bro, whenever you can get away from Cruella, holla at me," Nestaja said as she examined her new car. It was her favorite color – red - with soft peanut butter leather interior. With the new whip and gear, she was definitely ready to roll out for the evening. She walked over to Craz and gave him a big hug and kiss on the cheek. "Thank you so much, baby, I love it!"

"I knew you would. You know I know what you like."

"I wanna hit a few corners. Me and the car is just too cute to be sittin' doin' nothing. I'll be right back."

"Okay, babe, have fun and be safe," he said as he handed her his .9mm.

Katrina, Asia and Niko jumped in the car with Nestaja and they girls drove off, shining on the whole block, looking like a million dollars.

Chapter 7

After a long night, Nestaja decided to turn in for the evening. She wanted to thank Craz for the amazing gifts he showered her with, but she had a long day. Being fresh out of the hospital with no recovery time was starting to catch up with her. She dropped Niko, Katrina and Asia off, then went home to get some rest. Asia was feeling a little tipsy, but she wasn't ready to shut down for the night, so she decided to go pay her long term on again/off again boyfriend Jason a visit.

Asia and Jason were a hot item. They were the modern Bonnie and Clyde, which is how Asia caught her murder rap. She caught Jason at a restaurant with another woman, and she completely lost it. He tried to walk away without making a scene. Asia took it as him being disrespectful and reacted on her emotions. She pulled out her burner and popped on him. In the process, she shot an elderly man in the head, who died instantly. She fled the scene and got away. Thanks to Craz, she had a whole new identity, and the chances of her getting caught were very slim. There had been times when she would see him in traffic and they would end up on a high- speed shootout with each other, just to meet up later so they could hit each other off with some passionate thug love. Despite all the drama they went through, Jason loved Asia and would do any and everything for her. He bought her a house in Windsor Hills, paid cash for her new luxury car, and made sure she was well taken care of.

Once Asia arrived at Jason's house, she looked in her mirror to make sure her make-up and hair were on point. She got out and headed to the front door. As she approached the door, she heard music and laughter. She once had a key, but since she was still crazy in love with Jason and would sometime pop up and put out whatever company he had, he ended up changing the locks. Asia creeped around the house to peek through the window and saw him indulging in a threesome. He had a dark-skinned girl lying on her back, a light-skinned female orally pleasing her, and Jason was pounding the light-skinned girl from the back.

I know this muthafucka ain't getting down like this, she thought to herself. "He could have at least hooked up with some fly bitches. These hoes are busted," she mumbled, focusing on the cheap swap meet clothes on the floor next to a bottle of Taaka vodka. She knew her chances weren't that great, but she decided to go with the odds and knock on the door to see if he would answer. She walked back around to the front and rang the doorbell. No one answered, so she began to bang.

"Open this damn door, Jason!" she demanded. "Who is it?" he replied.

"You know who it is. Open the door before I kick it in." "Shit!" she heard him say.

"Who is that knocking on the door like that?" she heard one of the girls ask.

"It's my crazy-ass ex, and y'all need to get up outta here," Jason said as he put his clothes on, praying she didn't kick the door in.

"We ain't goin' nowhere!" the other female added.

"Well, bitch, you on your own," Jason snapped, causing them to indulge in a lightweight argument.

Asia was trying her best to get in and break up his little party. She walked around the house looking for something to bust the windows so she could get in. Then she realized that would be pointless, since he put bars on them. *I know he changed the locks on the house, but I know he didn't think to change the ones on his cars,* she thought as she headed to the garage. She popped the lock on the garage door. Good thing it was detached from the house so he didn't hear a thing. She decided against getting in his foreign luxury car. It wouldn't serve the purpose. She jumped in his big, freshly-custom-painted truck and slowly backed out of the garage without giving it any gas so the duals wouldn't sound. She aimed the truck directly toward his house and mashed on the gas full speed ahead, driving it right through his living room. She jumped out, a little off-balance from the impact of the truck hitting the house, but she shook it off and made her way through the debris, looking for him.

She went in his kitchen, where she found the light-skinned girl balled up in the corner ass-naked. Asia punched her a few times. "This is for those ugly-ass clothes layin' on the floor. Get some style, bitch!" she scolded.

Then she heard the back door slam, but when she made her way back there, all she could see was the back of Jason hopping over the wall, trying to get away to avoid her. She tried to chase after him, but her ankle was hurt from either the crash or trying to jump out of the monster truck in some stilettos. She grabbed her burner and started shooting over the gate, but it was too late. He had gotten away. She walked back in the kitchen to find the light-skinned girl still on the floor, crying hysterically. Asia looked her over than shook her head at the cheap jewelry, realizing she had nothing worth taking. Asia punched her up a little more and walked toward the bedroom, where she found the dark-skinned girl. But before Asia could say anything, WHAM! The girl hit her in the face with a shoe.

Did this bitch just hit me with a shoe? Asia thought, shaking it off. Asia hit her in the face with the butt of her gun, knocking her out cold. Angry that she didn't catch Jason, Asia headed to her car to avoid catching another case, since she had made a vow that she would only kill if she had to and not over any bullshit like this. Although the incident that had just taken place was enough to get her caught up, that was the least of her worries. She knew Jason would never snitch her out, and because the girls were dealing with him, she was more than sure they were aware of his hood rapport. They knew if they said anything to the police or anybody else, Jason himself would put them to rest. She got in her car and drove off a little upset because she really wanted to fuck him that night, but she was so turned on by what she had done to him and his little bitches that she was somewhat satisfied. On her way home, she stopped at the liquor store and got a box of blunts and a bottle of Patron. When she arrived at her house, she noticed a little black car in her driveway.

Whose car is this in my yard? she thought. She parked her car on the street in case she had to make a fast getaway. Once she got out, she decided to go through the back. When she got inside, she heard water running. She followed the sound of the running water, which led her upstairs to her bedroom. When she got up there, she realized it was the shower in her bathroom. She went in with her gun in hand, ready to shoot anything that moved. As she got closer to the shower, the male silhouette behind the frosted glass began to look familiar to her. She held her burner tighter as she walked up and opened the door to find Jason standing there wet, lathered up in soap, looking like the sexy hood star he was. She still held on to her gun since she didn't know what his intentions were.

"Put the gun down and get your ass in the shower," he demanded.

Now I know this nigga ain't acting like nothing just happened, she thought. *Why is he trying to get me in the shower with him?* "Hell no, nigga, all the soap in the world can't clean that dirty dick of yours!" She walked away with the gun in her hand, looking around her house for someone that he might have brought with him.

He got out and wrapped a towel around his nicely-cut chocolate body. He walked over to Asia and grabbed her. "Come here, bitch! You know it turns me on when you act out like that," he said as he began to tear her clothes off with one hand while pulling her hair with the other, attempting to stick his tongue down her throat.

Asia resisted, but this sexy Tyrese lookalike standing in front of her was just irresistible. "Jason, you wasn't with just one bitch. You was with two. I'm not fucking you," she said as she tried to push away.

"I had on a condom, and you know you want this dick. Why you trippin', boo?" "Fuck you, Jason!" she yelled as she made another attempt to get away.

But Jason just held her tighter. Once he got all her clothes off, he slammed her naked body on the bed, pinning her down with his sexy frame. "You know you want this dick, bitch!" he whispered while inserting his manhood inside her. He gently stroked her until she finally relaxed. Then he began to beat her pussy with his dick while grabbing her neck, whispering, "Bitch, you better not ever pull no shit like that again. Daddy takes good care of you, don't he?"

"Um-hmm." She could barely respond since he was so deep in her stomach.

"I can't hear you, bitch."

"Yeeess, daddeee!" "Tell me you love me!"

"I love you, daddy!" she said as she began to give it back to him.

He loosened up on her neck a little bit, but he continued to stroke her roughly until he reached his climax. Asia pushed him off her because she knew he was now tired and weak. Even though she enjoyed the rough sex, she couldn't let him know, so she started punching and slapping him, yelling about the situation.

"Nigga, you got me fucked up! Don't you ever get at me like that again, or it's gon' be problems."

Even though her punches had a powerful force, he was just too tired to argue with her. He knew it would only lead to more rough sex, and that's how he knew she liked it. He let her get away with it since there was no way he could go for a second round, so he agreed with her. "Okay, baby!"

Shortly after, Jason rolled over and went to sleep, Asia got up and went downstairs to clean up, and that's when she remembered he had come in an unfamiliar car. *That gotta be a bitch's car*, she thought.

She tiptoed upstairs to make sure he was sound asleep. She got the keys out of his pants pocket that were on her bathroom floor and headed outside. She opened the car door, and the first thing she noticed was a picture on the dash of him and a dark-skinned female that was halfway decent. She took a good look at the picture and realized it was the girl that hit her in the face with the shoe.

He must fuck with this bitch on a regular, she thought as she examined the picture a few seconds longer. She put the picture back on the dash like she had found it and continued to rummage through the car. She opened the glove compartment and noticed an envelope that read *FOR YOU CINNAMON BOO!* She opened it, and there was a large amount of money, all hundreds. She knew it was from Jason since she knew his writing and he would give her money the same way, in an envelope marked "Asia Boo". Of course she took it, along with a few other things to make it look like a break-in and not something she had done. She vandalized the car and left the door open to really make it look legit.

She headed back in the house and got in the bed, happy and anxious for Jason to get up and leave so she could count the money and go shopping. She forced herself to sleep so she could wake up and

Ghetto Diva

start a new financially blessed day.

Chapter 8

Ring…Ring…

"Who is this calling me this early in the morning?"

Ring…Ring…

"Hello?" Nestaja answered in an agitated tone. "Hey, babe!"

"What's up, Craz?"

"Just calling to see how my favorite girl in the whole wide world is doing this beautiful morning?"

Aggravated with his chipper tone, Nestaja responded, "I'm fine!"

"How you like your car?" he asked.

"I love it, baby, thanks for everything." Nestaja responded. "Anything for my baby."

"What are you doing today?" she asked.

"I don't have any plans until later this evening. Why, what's up?"

"Oh nothing, I just asked." Nestaja knew from his response that he wanted to kick it with her. She also knew that she still hadn't given him that special gift she promised him when he bailed her out of jail. She knew it was only right to thank him for all he had done. "Why don't you come over and get in this big comfy bed with me? I'm here all alone, and I'm scared the boogie man might come get me," she said in her flirty, seductive voice.

"Okay, babe, I'll be there in about thirty minutes," he responded.

"I'll see you when you get here."

"Have you checked your mailbox?" he asked.

"Can you check it for me when you get here?" she answered. "No, baby, I need you to check it before I get there. I - ”

He was interrupted by a call coming in on her other line, so she rushed him off the phone.

“Okay, babe, I’ll check it in a minute. See you when you get here.”

“Okay!” he responded and then hung up.

“Hello?” she answered.

“Hey, biootch!” a friendly voice sang through the phone. “Hey, Simone, when did you get back from Belize?”

“I got back yesterday.”

“How was your trip?” Nestaja asked.

“It was cool. You know I’m just trying to stay occupied until my nigga come home. So what’s been going on while I been gone?”

Simone was one of Nestaja’s best friends, but one she didn’t see as often as she did the others. They mostly talked on the phone. They had met at Southwest College a few years ago.

Simone was kind of a homebody and didn’t come out that often. She hooked up with one of Nestaja’s cousins a few summers ago when Nestaja first met Craz, and they would all hang out sometimes. When Simone stopped talking to Nestaja’s cousin, she went back into hibernation until she met Dada. She found her true love and married him, but a year after they got married, he caught a case and had to do five years, so she went back on lockdown.

Nestaja was giving Simone the rundown on what had gone on the past two months that she was gone. There was so much to be said that time was lost, and Nestaja noticed an hour and twenty minutes had passed and Craz had not gotten there yet. She also forgot to check the

mailbox, so she stepped outside to get the mail. In there was an envelope that read “For the most beautiful girl in the world. Enjoy.” She opened it and found ten paper-clipped thousand dollar stacks inside with a note that read “shopping money”. She was so happy, she let out a loud scream.

“Damn, bitch, what’s wrong with you?” Simone asked.

“Girl, Craz has been outdoing himself, showering me with all kind of gifts and money. He gave me a party, brought me seven complete expensive name brand outfits with matchin’ shoes and bags, a brand new luxury SUV, and I just looked in my mailbox and he gave me $10,000 to shop with."

"All I wanna know is, what you gon' do when S Man comes home?"

"What you mean? Ain't nothing gonna come between me and S Man. That's my Clyde, my Malcolm. I'm Camille to his Bill. Our love is unbreakable."

"Whatever, bitch. You're going to fuck around and lose a good man."

"No, I'm not, because I'm going to always keep it 100 with S Man. I tell him everything, because I refuse to let him hear anything from someone else."

"Well, what are you going to do about Craz when S Man gets out? You really think that nigga is going to let you go that easy after he bought you all this expensive shit? I guess you're going to have S Man driving the car that Craz got you, Ms. Pimp. I bet you didn't think about that, did you?"

"Well, he can't take the car back. It's in my name. Niko hooked him up with it, but she made sure his name was nowhere on it. My name is on the title; therefore, it's my car."

"Okay, bitch, and you wonder why these niggas be trying to kill your ass when it's over.

Look at how you do 'em."

"Whaaaat?" Nestaja whined.

"You be fuckin 'em, suckin' 'em, and then you think you can leave when you don't want to deal with 'em no more, after they have thanked you in more ways than one just to keep your silly ass near."

"Awww, bitch…" Nestaja's doorbell rang. "Okay, Simone, Craz is here. Let me fuck and suck him and I'll call you later."

"Bye, hoe!" Simone replied.

Nestaja hung up and headed to the door with just her stilettos and ¾ inch silk designer robe on. When she opened the door, Craz instantly grabbed her and began to caress her all over her body with his talented tongue. He led her to the living room and laid her on her ivory European leather sofa. Since she was a squirter, that was a big no-no. She resisted because she didn't want to get any cum stains on her expensive sofa that she had shipped directly from Europe. She tried to lead him to the bedroom, but he was feeling it and he wanted to get down right there.

"No, let's go to the room!" she whispered.

"Uh-uh!" he responded while he continued to orally please her.

She was enjoying it, but was trying hard to ignore the feeling, not wanting to get anything on her sofa. She tried to pull away, but he was so into what he was doing he didn't stop. She looked around to see what she could grab to ease under herself, but the living room was a room that wasn't used often, and there was nothing in sight. She couldn't use her robe because it was silk and it would go right through. She managed to grab his shirt, but with her sudden movement, his finger inside her, and his tongue on her clit, he hit her spot. Squish! She squirted everywhere.

"Ummmmm, ummm!" she moaned.

She was a little upset that she came on her couch, but could no longer ignore the feeling. She snatched his clothes off and took his manhood into her juicy mouth. She worked the head, using some tongue and lip action, then she slowly worked her way down until the head was deep in her throat. She lifted his balls with her hand, pleasing them with her tongue while his head was still deep in her throat. She was good at what she did, and this was one thing that Craz loved. She didn't do it often, but he had messed up her expensive couch. She wouldn't feel right asking him to pay for it, so she knew exactly how to make him offer. He fought her since he didn't want to cum without going inside her, but she really wasn't feeling all that, so she continued to suck, lick, and deep throat his well-endowed penis until he reached his climax.

"No, Nestaja, stop, please! I don't want to cum yet. Please!"

But she continued until he came. She would usually swallow, but this time she spit it back on his dick and she slowly jacked it off, but it only got softer. She knew exactly what she was doing. There was something about her that would always drain him. He would usually have tons of stamina and could go for hours. But she knew just what to do to break him down. Even when he could go for a long time, once he busted one nut with her, he was no good for at least a few hours, and that's just what she wanted. So, she got up, got a towel, and made an attempt to clean up the mess she made.

He stopped her and said, "Don't worry about it, I'll order you another one tomorrow."

Yes! My plan worked, she thought. "Are you hungry?" she asked. "Yeah!"

She rushed to the kitchen to make some homemade smothered potatoes, scrambled eggs with onions and cheese, biscuits, and turkey sausage with freshly-squeezed orange juice. The two sat at the table and enjoyed a nice breakfast, then watched a movie. Shortly after the movie was off, she figured out a way to rush him off so she could start her day. With all that extra money in her purse, she was ready to go shopping.

Chapter 9

"Hello?" Asia answered her phone. "What's up, Asia?"

"Hey, what's up, Crystal, what you got going on?" Asia asked. "Girl, this muthafucka got me so fucked up!"

"What's wrong, Cris?"

"Michael didn't come home last night. I want you to go with me on a mission," Crystal cried.

"Okay, I'm on the way!" Asia responded.

"No, I'm coming to get you, because the bitch he fuckin' with lives by you. I'll be there in about twenty minutes."

Crystal rushed to her room to put something on that would make her look presentable, but comfortable. She brushed her hair back in a nice and sleek ponytail and threw on a cute sweatsuit. She looked in the mirror to make sure everything was up to par. The outfit was hugging every curve just right and made her booty look delicious. She didn't need to do much since she displayed a natural beauty. She had a smooth yellow skin tone with light green eyes. She stood about 5'9" and weighed 165 pounds, with long pretty legs, a 28-inch waist, and a firm 38-DD cup size to complete the package.

She went outside, contemplating if she should take her car or his. Following her first impulse, she jumped in his. Not knowing what was about to happen, she didn't want to take any chances and mess up hers.

When she arrived, Asia was already sitting on the porch waiting. She got in the car and Crystal sped off. Asia fired up a blunt and took three pulls on it. As she reached for the ashtray to put it out, Crystal stopped her.

"No! Don't put it out, let me hit it." "Crystal, you don't smoke."

"Well, I need it now to relax my mind, because right now I'm about ready to blow my baby daddy's brains out," Crystal replied, waving her 9-millimeter in the air.

"Here, bitch, hurry up and hit it," Asia said as she quickly passed her the blunt. "God knows I don't need you killing nobody."

Crystal took a long hard pull on the blunt.

"Damn, Cris, that ain't no dick, let it go. You ain't no weed smoker. You can't handle taking a hit like that, girl, this some of that fire," Asia said as she handed Crystal a bottle of water to help with the choking.

"Dayaaamn!" Crystal managed to say in between coughs, feeling like her chest was about to cave in and her insides were coming out.

"See, you hit it too hard. I don't know what you and Nestaja be thinking. Don't either one of y'all bitches smoke, but when that once every two-year time come around, y'all wanna hit it like you been doing it for years. This is a blunt, not a dick. You don't suck it; you hit it," Asia said in a joking way.

As they pulled up to their destination, Crystal noticed Michael's other car sitting out front. She rushed out of the car while Asia checked the surroundings. Crystal knew Michael wasn't going to allow his little hood rat to open the door and she didn't want to break in. She just wanted him to come out, so she climbed on the hood of his truck and started jumping until the alarm went off. About twenty seconds later, Michael came out with his chrome .45 in his hand and a short, light-skinned female running behind.

"What the fuck are you doing?" Michael screamed.

"Oh, this is what you're out doing while I'm at home taking care of our two kids? You do remember them, don't you? And who is this poor little thing standing behind you?"

"You're tripping, Crystal, this somebody I do business with. She's my booster. How you think I be coming home with all that stuff for you and the kids?" he said while walking up to his truck that she was still jumping on.

"Oh, I'm just your booster, Michael? I take penitentiary chances stealing shit for you, and you're taking it to another bitch that I didn't know nothing about?"

"Shut up, KeKe!" he yelled.

"No, let her talk, Michael," Crystal said as she flopped down on the hood. "Hell no! And if you don't get yo' ass off my truck, I'ma shoot you."

"Nigga, you ain't the only one with heat out here," she said as she cocked her nine. "Since y'all wanna play with guns, let me go get my shit," KeKe said as she turned around, making an attempt to go in the house. But before she made it inside, she ended up getting hit in the chin by Asia, which knocked her out cold. Asia took all her jewelry off and put it in her pocket.

"Man, y'all can't be coming over people's houses starting shit," Michael said, shocked at what Asia had done.

"No, Michael, you started this shit when you started fucking with this bitch."

"Crystal, I told you, I don't fuck with her. Now get your ass off my truck. I'm not going to tell you again."

"Hell nah, I'm not getting off. It's in my name, so it's mine. You need to be checking on your little chicken-head bitch that my homegirl just knocked out," Crystal said as she stood up on the hood again.

"I don't give a fuck about that bitch. I told you, it was just business. Now get your ass off my shit, Crystal. I'm not playing with your yellow ass," Michael said as he cocked his gun.

"No!" Crystal said as she stood on her tiptoes, which caused the hood to dent in.

"Bitch, get yo' ass down now!" he said, aiming his .45 at her foot while thinking about the $2500 he had spent on the paint.

She aimed her .9mm and got off two shots and so did he, hitting her in the left foot. "Nigga, you fucked up my designer tennis shoes!" she said as she hopped off the truck, trying not to stand on the foot he had just shot. "Michael, what's wrong with you?" she asked as she hopped up on him, noticing that he had blood on his shoulder.

"I'm calling the police," KeKe mumbled as she began to regain consciousness.

"No, you not, bitch!" Michael yelled. "You got all that stolen shit in your house, girl. Call 'em if you want to and you'll be the one going to jail, not me or my girl."

"You choosing this hoe over me, Michael?"

"Bitch, you was just a fuck, and you was good for what you was good for," Crystal stated.

"I'ma have my brother fuck you up, Michael!" KeKe screamed.

"Bitch, shut up before I have my homegirl knock your ass out again," Michael said as he beckoned for Asia to come back over there.

"I'm not scared of that bitch. She just caught me off-guard."

"Oh, I caught you off-guard?" Asia replied as she positioned herself to get down with her.

The two started fighting, but KeKe couldn't hang, so she gave up.

"Michael, you and your baby momma is crazy! Just stay the fuck away from me," she said as she tried to catch her breath, walking around looking for her jewelry, which Asia had already pocketed. "Don't come nowhere near me, Michael. I don't know your name, girl, but I didn't know he had a family."

"Whatever, bitch!" Crystal said as she limped back to the car. "Bitch, where you think you going?" Michael asked.

"I'm going to the hospital."

"No, you not! Give Asia the keys to that car. You coming with me. You shot me too, bitch, so we're about to ride this shit out together. Get yo' yellow ass in the truck."

"I'm not going nowhere with you, Michael."

"Bitch, get in the truck!" he said as he grabbed her by the back of the head with his good arm and forced her in the truck.

Crystal and Michael had been together since they were teenagers. They had two beautiful children. The only reason they weren't married was because Crystal felt he wasn't ready. He still had some growing up to do. They both knew they would always be together, regardless of all the fights, shootouts, and drama they had been through with each other. They were still in love and would never let anything come between them.

Michael got in the truck and hollered out the window to Asia, "Take the car to the house, and Crystal will call you after my shoulder heals up."

Ghetto Diva

Asia laughed, because this was something Michael and Crystal always went through. They would have the craziest fights, and five minutes after it was over, they would be back talking like nothing ever happened. But Asia could relate, because she and Jason went through the same thing.

On the way to the hospital, Michael and Crystal rolled with the sounds of Kendrick Lamar subbing so loud it was vibrating everything on the truck. When the song went off, Michael turned it down.

"Babe, don't you think we're getting too old for this shit?"

Crystal looked at him as she wrapped her foot with a towel she found in his truck. "Why you say that?"

"Look, Crystal, we've been together damn near all our lives. We know we're right for each other."

"Okay, and…?" Crystal sarcastically responded. "Baby, I think it's time we get married."

"Nigga, I just caught you at a bitch's house not even fifteen minutes ago, and now you talking about marriage. I keep telling you, you're not ready, Michael."

"Yes, I am!" he replied as he took her hand. "Let's focus on just us for the next year and we'll get married the summer after that," he said as he caressed her hand.

"So what are you asking from me, Michael?"

"I'm saying I love you! I already know I'm going to spend the rest of my life with you. So let's do it right. We can go to premarital counseling. I'll work on my flaws and you work on yours. No more shooting at each other and fighting from this point on. Crystal, will you marry me?" Michael asked as he kissed her hand.

"Yes, baby, I will. But we have to work hard on our flaws. And can you please hurry up and get me to the hospital? My damn foot hurts! And what are we gonna tell them when we get there?"

"We're gonna tell them we got caught in the crossfire of a drive-by shooting." "Okay, baby, sorry 'bout that shoulder."

"It's okay, it didn't go in. It just skinned me a little bit. But I'm sorry about your foot." "Well, it didn't skin me, it went in. You owe me some new shoes and a bag."

"A bag?" Michael asked.

"Yeah, for the pain and suffering I endured." "Okay, babe, you got that coming."

Chapter 10

"Look, DJ, I'm not feeling you and haven't been for some years now. That's why the kids and I are moving," Katrina said as she loaded her car with all of hers and her kids' belongings.

"But Katrina, I give you everything. You don't have to work or pay bills. You dress in the finest clothes, have the jewels, and drive the best cars."

"DJ, don't make it like I don't get out and hustle and bring money into this house too. I paid for my own clothes."

"Katrina, when you chose to dance at the club, I didn't say shit. I just let you do you, even though I didn't want you to."

"Well, I'm still doin' me and I'm moving."

"What is it, Katrina? I'll boost your weekly allowance to $4000 instead of the $2000. Or do you want me to buy us a bigger house?"

"The house in Baldwin Hills is 4800 square feet with a pool, and I got it for me and my kids, so buying me a house ain't it. It's you as a person. I don't like nothing about you. I hate the way you walk, smell, talk, dress. I just don't love you no more, and I'm tired of faking like I do. I even hate that damn football team you coach for, and the one you watch on TV."

"What house in Baldwin Hills?" DJ questioned.

But Katrina cut him off. "Ain't nothing you can do, so stop trying. And you're still going to give me my weekly allowance, because I need it to take care of my three kids."

"What house in Baldwin Hills?" DJ asked again.

"Me and the kids found a place in Baldwin Hills, DJ, so just do you and get over it, because I'm not coming back."

"Oh, you must be suckin' some nigga dick good, he puttin' you in houses and shit. I know dancing in that club damn sure won't get you a house in Baldwin Hills. And I bet he was the one that sent you all those roses. That didn't come from your auntie as a thank you for taking care of her, did it?"

"Look, DJ, it don't matter. I'm leaving. It's over. So you can go fuck with whatever bitch you want to. I don't have to worry about you coming home when you feel like it, and I don't have to worry about you always bringing your homies with you when you do decide to come home."

"You better hope karma gets to you before I do, because bitch, you're going to pay for hurting me like this."

"Whatever, DJ! That's the least of my worries. You not tryna kill nothing or let nothing die, so stop poking your chest out and move so I can get outta the driveway."

"You not goin' nowhere, Katrina."

"DJ, I don't want to run your little ass over, so move away from my door so I can go." "Bitch, I'ma kick your ass when I catch you!"

Katrina jumped out of her car and DJ made an attempt to slap her, but she caught his hand in mid-swing and said, "DJ, did you forget? You can't fight."

"Katrina, please, just give me a chance, baby. I don't want to fight. I just want my family. Why you gotta listen to them hoes you kick it with every day?" DJ said as he wiped the tears from his eyes.

"Hell no! I gave you chance after chance. I don't love you no more, DJ. It's over. I have no feelings for you at all, and I wish you would stop saying it's my friends. Nobody has anything to do with this move but me."

"Well, you're not takin' my son," DJ said as he walked over to the car, trying to take his son out.

"DJ, please! You don't run shit, so get away from the car before I do something to you in front of your son."

"Bitch, I know them so-called friends and cousins of yours hooked you up with somebody, and you think it's gonna be better with him. But when that nigga starts treating you like shit and going upside your head, don't come calling me, because I hope he dog your ass out."

"Well, if he do, at least I know I can walk away with way more than I'm walking away with now while leaving your dusty ass."

"Katrina, let's talk!"

"What is there to talk about, DJ? Look, let me give you some advice so you can make it work with the next bitch. Go take a bath and get yourself together, and maybe you'll find a decent girl to put up with your bullshit. Just don't get comfortable like you did with me, and maybe she'll stay."

"Katrina, is it somebody else?"

"Okay, DJ, you want to know the truth? Well, here it is. Yes, there is another nigga, and he makes me feel like a woman. See, your ass was too busy in the streets to even realize that I've been cheating. He's been around for a year now and we're goin' to Las Vegas in a few weeks to get married. Now there is the truth. Can you handle it?"

DJ hauled off and punched Katrina in the face. "Bitch, you been playing me all this time? So, this nigga is the one that's been having you come in at 4:00 and 5:00 in the morning? It never was your cousins, was it?"

Katrina couldn't answer because she was too focused on her mouth, which was bleeding from the hit. She couldn't believe he had actually hit her.

"Yeah, bitch, I did that!" DJ said as he bounced around like he was in a boxing ring. "Tell your nigga to come holla at me."

"You know what, DJ? I'ma let that slide, because I know you're working on some emotional bullshit."

"Nah, bitch, tell your new nigga to come holla at me. He owes me a lot of money."

"DJ, nobody owes you shit!"

"Watch your back in traffic! I'ma have my little homegirls looking for you."

"DJ, I'm not hard to find. Tell all them bitches if they want me, they know where I be and to come holla at me and we can deal with the situation however. It's nothing."

"Oh, you think you hard?"

"No, DJ, you think I'm hard," Katrina said as she snickered and got in her car. She drove off, leaving DJ standing in the driveway looking like a lost puppy.

"I can't believe she did this to me!" DJ shouted as he walked inside his now-empty home.

Had he waited a little longer to come home, he would have really been clueless as to what was going on. The movers had already taken everything to Katrina's new house earlier that morning after DJ had left. The only things that were left behind were his clothes, a 25-inch TV, and a trashcan. When he arrived, she was putting some of hers and the kids' things in her car.

As DJ stood in the middle of the once plushed-out living room, he thought, *My safe!* He immediately ran to the backyard. When he saw that the doghouse had been moved, he already knew she took the money that was buried under the doghouse. Not only did she take everything in the house, but she took his life savings too - ten years of hustling, all gone in an instant.

***

Once Katrina got on the freeway, heading to her new home in Baldwin Hills, she started to feel a little bad for what she had done. *I been so unhappy these past few years being with DJ, so why should I feel bad?* she thought as she fired up her kush blunt. *Besides, Deshon treats me and these kids like we're supposed to be treated. He buys me flowers, he makes sure we all have what we need, and he got a promising future. DJ thinks he can live off of selling drugs the rest of his life. I'd rather be happy and comfortable than be unhappy and miserable.* She also knew that she could get away with it, because DJ wasn't the type that would retaliate. He was a hustler, but more so a good college boy gone bad. He was raised in an upscale neighborhood, got accepted to a university on a football scholarship, but was later kicked out for selling drugs on campus.

Her thoughts were interrupted by her cell phone vibrating on her hip.

"Hello?" she answered.

"Katrina, baby!" an elderly voice said on the other end. "Hey, Grandma," Katrina responded.

"I got Gina on the other line. She wanted me to call you on this three-way thing, so you hold on, baby, you know I don't know how to work all this new stuff."

"Okay, Grandma, just hit the flash button and it should put us all together." "Okay, baby."

"Hello?"

"Hey, cousin!"

"Hey, Gina! When are you coming home?"

"I get out next week, and I need you to pick me up." "Okay, cousin, I'll come get you. Where exactly are you?"

"I'm up here in Chowchilla. It's about thirty miles north of Fresno." "I'll be there!" Katrina responded.

"What's up with the rest of the crew?"

"Everybody fine. We'll update you on all the gossip and goodies when you get out," Katrina responded.

"That's what's up! I been down for four years and I'm coming home to nothing, so I'm going to need y'all to look out for me when I first get home. You know me. It won't be long before I get back on my feet."

"Gina, don't trip, we don't want you getting into any more trouble, so we got you." "Okay. I got to go; my time is up. Tell the girls that I love them, and I'll see y'all next

week!"

"Love you too!" Katrina responded and released the line with a smile on her face.

Gina was their cousin. She had gone to jail four years ago. She went to rob a local gambling shack that was set up behind a gas station, but the lick went bad. She made an attempt to flee the scene, but as she came through the gas station, she slipped in some oil, her burner slid across the floor, and the owner hit the panic button. She got charged with attempted robbery with possession of a firearm. Since she had never been in any trouble and had a lot of support from her family, her lawyer was able to get her three years on the robbery and one year on the gun with three years parole.

Katrina immediately called Asia to tell her the good news.

"Hello!" Asia answered in a very happy voice, like this was one of the best days of her life.

"Damn, bitch, you must have got some real good dick last night!"

"Hell nah! But I'm up an extra ten grand."

"Well, good, because Gina just called, and she's coming home next week. You know she don't have anything."

"I'm on my way to the Beverly Center, so meet me up there so we can grab her a few fly 'fits," Asia responded.

"Okay. Let me drop my kids off to Grandma. I'll hit you when I get up there so you can tell me exactly where you are."

"Okay, but hurry up, because I got a pocket full of money and I'm ready to spend, spend, spend!" Asia happily said.

"Okay!" Katrina replied, before releasing the call.

Chapter 11

Thank God he's gone. Now I can get dressed and go shopping. I know he'll do anything for me. I'm really starting to not like Craz at all. It's not his looks, and it's sure not the sex.

Maybe it's the fact that he thinks he's playing me. Hmmm, what he don't know is that I'm fully aware of all of his lil side chicks. Oh well, none of them hoes will ever walk in my red bottoms, Nestaja thought as she slid on her sandals with her sexy strapless white summer dress, and a smile on her face. Just as she went to grab her matching bag and head out the door, her house phone rang, so she raced to the kitchen to answer it.

"Hello?"

"Hi, Mommy!" Jasmine said in a very excited voice. "Hey princess, what are you doing?"

"Nothing, Mommy. Me and Josiah want to come home."

"Jasmine, I promise, you and Josiah will be home real soon. Where are y'all?" "At grandma's stinky friend's house," Jasmine replied sadly.

"Don't worry, baby, you're in good hands with your grandma. I'm going to be coming to get y'all real soon. Where is Josiah?"

"Right here!" Jasmine said as she gave her brother the phone. "Hello?"

"What's up, son?"

"Mama, I'm ready to come home."

"I know, and I'm ready for you to come home. I miss y'all so much, but you know how Reggie can be. I just have to play this out right."

"But Mama, you're smarter than him."

"I know, but this time we have legal issues, so I have to do this right. You do understand, don't you?"

"Yeah, I do!"

"I'm so happy to hear yours and Jasmine's voices, you just don't now." "Mama, something is wrong with Jasmine. She be peeing on herself."

"She do?" Nestaja replied in shock. *Jasmine hasn't peed on herself since she been potty trained. This situation is messing with my baby in more ways than one. I gotta get my kids now.* Nestaja thought. "Josiah, where are y'all?

"We're at Grandma's friend's house. She lives down the street from a school called Centennial, but we're on a street called Parmalee. We have to go to her son's birthday party today. Mama, I don't want to be at this party. They just have hot dogs, ice cream, cake, and some cheap soda."

"I'm sure it's not that bad, Josiah."

"Mama, they don't have a jumper or nothing. All they have for the party is each other." "You know how to make the best of it for you and Jasmine. I know this is something that

y'all are not used to, but trust me, son, it's just temporary. Just call me every chance y'all get. I'm going to get y'all home real soon, don't trip. And Josiah, I need you to be strong for Jasmine. You know she is only peeing on herself because of the situation. When this is all over and done with, we are going to pack up and move away from everybody. Make sure you hug Jasmine every night and tell her you love her, and that Mommy does too. And when she hug you back, that's me telling you I love you."

"Okay, Mama!"

"Now get off the phone before your grandma comes in and sees you on it. I don't want her to suspect nothing."

"She's not here. She went to San Diego to pick up somebody. We're here with her friend Norma getting ready for the party."

"Is the party there?" "Yes!" Josiah answered.

"You said it's on a street called Parmalee, right?" Nestaja asked. "Yes!"

"I got the number on my caller ID, so I will get the address. I'm coming to get y'all today. What time does the party start?"

"It's some people here now." "A lot of people?" she asked "Kinda!" Josiah responded.

"Is the party in the front or the back?" "In the back," Josiah answered.

"Well, you and Jasmine stay close to the front. Make sure you keep Jasmine close to you, and when you see Cousin Tyrone's car, you and Jasmine come get in. You hear me?"

"Yeah, Mama."

"I'll see y'all in a little bit." Nestaja hung up the phone and picked it back up to call information.

"Directory Assistance, city and state please." "Compton, California!"

"Your listing please?"

"The Pizza Joint on Central," Nestaja responded.

"Please hold for your number. Your call to area code 310-555-8458 will be connected at no additional charge."

"Thank you for calling The Pizza Joint, will this be for delivery or carry out?" "Delivery!" Nestaja responded.

"Can I have your home telephone number, please? "310-555-4515!"

"Norma Jenkins at 2110 N. Parmalee?"

"Yes. I would like to order twenty large pizzas, all twenty with different toppings. It's for a party."

"No problem, ma'am, but since this is such a large order, I'm going to need you to prepay with a credit card, or come in and pay with cash."

"Okay, if I come in and pay will your driver still deliver?" Nestaja asked. "Most definitely!" the female on the phone answered.

"Okay, I'll be there shortly."

"Okay ma'am. I'm not supposed to do this, but I'm going to go ahead and put the order in so it can be ready when you get here."

"Oh, thank you!" Nestaja said. She hung up the phone and called her cousin Tyrone. "What's up!" he answered.

"Hey cousin, I need a huge favor." "What's up, Nestaja?"

"I need you to take me to Compton to grab the kids from this little party," Nestaja said.

"Okay, cousin. I'm right down the street from you with this lil broad I be messing with, so let me drop her ass off, and I'll be there in about ten minutes."

"Okay, see you when you get here." She hung up and ran in her room to change her clothes. She looked in her mirror and decided not to change. *This is going to be easy,* she thought. She went outside and waited on Tyrone to pull up. While waiting, her cell phone rang.

"Hello?" she answered.

"Hey, what's up, Nestaja, this is Taj." "Hey girl, how are you?" Nestaja asked.

"I'm good. I was just calling to check on you since I hadn't heard from you."

"I'm okay. I been through a lot since I left that hellhole. I got jumped and a whole lot of other stuff. I don't really have time to go into details, but…"

"Girl, I been through a lot too," Taj said, cutting her off. "How about we do lunch next week?" Taj asked.

"That's fine with me." Nestaja responded.

"I told my mom about your case and she said it's a very weak case and she will take it, since you're a friend. She usually doesn't take such small cases because she likes a challenge," Taj said with a giggle. "She asked me to get your information so she can look further into it."

"No problem," Nestaja said. "My booking number is E112927, and my name is Nestaja Simmons, N-E-S-T-A-J-A and my date of birth is 11/20/89."

"Ummmm, a freaky-ass Scorpio!" Taj said in a joking way. "Don't go there, Taj," Nestaja added.

"I'm not! I know you love men. But I'm going to call her and give her your information.

I'll call you in a few days, and we can decide where and when we're going to meet." "Okay!" Nestaja said, disconnecting the call while getting in the car with her cousin. "What's up, cousin?" Tyrone said as he drove off.

"You know the situation with Reggie and the kids, right? Reggie's mom went to San Diego and left my kids with her friend that lives on Parmalee. I need you to make one stop before we get there."

"Okay, where we need to stop?" Tyrone asked. "The Pizza Joint!" Nestaja responded.

"The Pizza Joint? Damn, cousin, you hungry or something?" "No, fool, just stop by there."

"Awwww shit, I know my cousin and you are up to something." "Well, not really," Nestaja responded.

"I'm not trippin', cousin, just tell me, Are we about to rob the place?" Tyrone asked. "Hell no! Those days are long over. Just pull up to the Pizza Joint and trust me, nigga. I wouldn't put you in fucked up situation," Nestaja added.

When they got to the Pizza Joint, Nestaja jumped out, went in, and paid for the pizzas. "Is it going to be long before the driver delivers?" she asked the cashier.

"No, he's loading up his car now," the cashier responded.

"I would like to give him a tip. Can you call him to the front, please?" Nestaja asked. "Sure. José!" the cashier called. "Come to the front. The customer with the large order has something for you."

José came to the front and Nestaja gave him a 100-dollar bill.

"I'm going to follow you to the party, but I don't want the people at the party to see me or know anything about who paid for the pizzas," Nestaja said as she gave him another 100- dollar bill.

"My lips are sealed," José said with a huge smile on his face as he walked to his car. Nestaja headed back to Tyrone's car and said, "Follow that beat-up Toyota pickup. "What the hell do you got going on, cousin?" Tyrone asked as he followed truck.

"I ordered pizzas because Josiah said there was no food there. I know twenty unexpected pizzas from Pizza Joint will be a big distraction to a low-budget bitch like Norma. The kids will be able to get in the car without anyone noticing," Nestaja said.

"Nestaja, you's a fool, but I gots ta give it to you, you got mad game," Tyrone commented while laughing, trying to keep up with the truck.

Nestaja's cell phone rang. "Hello?" she answered. "Bitch! Where you at?" Asia asked.

"In traffic with Tyrone. What's up?"

"Tell my cousin let's smoke something later." "Tyrone, Asia said smoke something later." "Tell her that's what's up and to get at me." "He said call him," Nestaja said to Asia.

"Tell him…"

"Now look, I'm not going to be relaying no messages. What's up, Asia?" "Damn, bitch!" Asia responded. "You got some money?" Asia asked. "Don't I always?"

"Aw, bitch, don't act like times don't get hard."

"Yeah, they do, but the designer bags have been on fat lately," Nestaja said in a sarcastic tone.

"Well, me and Katrina are meeting up at the Beverly Center in a little bit. You rollin' with us or not?" Asia asked.

"Yeah, I'll hit you when I'm on the way."

"Okay, and tell my cousin I'm going to call him. Bye!"

Nestaja hung up as they approached Norma's house. The pizza man got out of his truck and headed to the back where the party was going on. Nestaja saw the front door open, and out came Jasmine and Josiah.

"Mommy!" Jasmine screamed.

"Shhhhh! Come on y'all, get in the car." The kids got in the car and they drove off. "Hey, big girl!" Nestaja said to Jasmine.

"Mommy, we missed you," Jasmine said.

Nestaja leaned over the seat and kissed Jasmine on the cheek and grabbed Josiah's head and kissed him on the forehead.

"I missed y'all too."

"What's up, Tyrone?" Josiah said. "What's up, man, y'all straight?"

"Yeah, I don't want to ever go back with them again, Mama."

"And you won't. I'm going to call Child Services and let them know I want y'all in my family's custody, and that way we won't have any problems with the courts."

"Mommy, can we go somewhere?" Jasmine asked.

"How about we get in our brand new car and go shopping with Auntie Asia and Katrina?"

"Yeaaaah!" Jasmine responded.

"Mama, we got a new car?" Josiah asked. "We sure do. Craz got it for us."

"Can we get on the airplane and go somewhere?" Jasmine asked. "Where you wanna go, big girl?"

"I want to go somewhere so my daddy don't fight you no more and Josiah don't beat him up."

Nestaja looked at Tyrone as she said to Jasmine, "Baby, we're not going to fight anymore.

Your daddy is in jail, and I'm sure he will be there a few more months."

"No he not, Mama, he is getting out in a few days. I heard Grandma tell Norma that the jail is crowded and he only have to do three weeks," Josiah said.

"When did you hear her say this?" Nestaja asked. "About two weeks ago," Josiah responded.

"Cousin, don't trip. Just murk the nigga. You'll beat it, because you got paperwork on him."

"Yeah, I'll beat the case, but I might lose my kids due to my criminal behavior," Nestaja responded. "I'm going to figure out something. Thanks, Tyrone! We're going to go to the mall. Shopping will take our minds off all this drama," Nestaja said as she and the kids got out of Tyrone's car.

"All right. Now if you need me, call me," Tyrone replied. "Okay, cousin. I will."

"Bye, Tyrone!" Jasmine said.

"Whose car is this, Mama?" Josiah asked. "That's our new car."

"Wheeeew, all I see is shiny rims." Jasmine complimented. "Craz got this for us, Mama?" Josiah asked.

"Yes, he did!"

"He's all right with me. Mama, you should marry him," Josiah added.

"He's cool, but he ain't that damn cool. Now y'all go inside and change into some fresh gear so we can go hang out for a while. Hurry up so we can get a head start while it's still early. The sooner we go, the more we can do."

"Okay!" the kids said while making their way in the house.

Nestaja picked up her cell phone and dialed her sister. "Hello?" Asia answered. "Where are y'all?" Nestaja asked.

"We're pulling into the Beverly Center now." "Okay, we're on the way."

"Who's we?" Asia asked. "Me, Josiah, and Jasmine."

"How you get them?" Asia asked in an excited tone.

"I put my hood hand down, but I know they are going to come looking for them, so I'm going to get a room for now then send them to Momma until it's time for us to go to court," Nestaja said to Asia.

"I miss my niece and nephew. Y'all hurry up."

"Okay, I'll call you when we get outside."

Nestaja went inside and packed a bag for the next few days, and she and the kids headed out to the Beverly Center.

Chapter 12

Who in the hell is calling me at 6:30 in the morning? Nestaja thought as she leaned over to answer her phone. "Yeah!" she answered.

"Heeeey biiiotch!"

"Damn, Simone, do you ever sleep past 5:00 a.m.?" Nestaja asked, rolling out of her bed.

"Girl, it's Saturday and I can't go visit Dada because they're on lockdown," Simone said in an angry tone.

"So what that gotta do with me? Why do I have to suffer because you can't play with your nigga dick under the table?" Nestaja joked.

"Aww, bitch, fuck you! So what's been going on, Ms. Nestaja?"

"Girl, everything's been cool these past few days. Child Services gave me the okay to send my kids to Arizona with my mom. Craz has been working twelve hour shifts six days a week and hustling, so I haven't really been seeing him. The girls are fine - as a matter of fact, we're all getting together at Akira's house tonight. You wanna come hang out with us?"

"Nestaja, I don't know, I'm not really feeling it," Simone said in a depressed tone. "When do you ever feel it? You need to get out sometimes."

"Nah, I'm good. I'm going to stay here with the kids and watch some movies." Simone sighed.

"Girl, your life is so boring since Dada caught his case," Nestaja added. "Speaking of case, what's going on with your baby daddy?" Simone asked.

"I haven't heard anything, and really don't care to. When I got my kids, Josiah said he overheard Ms. Salazar saying he's getting out in a few weeks, and that was like three weeks ago."

"Well, you better be careful. You know he's still in love with you. There's no telling what he might do."

"Simone, I'm not worried about Reggie. The best revenge is to be kind and successful." "Yeah, you're going to successfully lock your lips around his dick!"

"Girl, please!"

"Nestaja, I been your friend for too long. You still love Reggie."

"I never said I didn't love him. If it wasn't for all the abuse and disrespect, I would still be with him. But he has too many anger issues."

"Well, you know there is anger management classes he can take," Simone replied. "Simone, I wouldn't give a damn what kind of class he takes. It's over with me and

Reggie. When he does come back around, I'm going to let my kindness kill him so I can get him where I want him, then I'ma gut punch that ass."

"Yeah, that kindness in your pussy that he loves so much? What you need to do is let me hit him with one of these Belizean spells, and I guarantee you won't have to worry about Mr.

Reggie's ass no more. He will be eating out of the palm of your hand." "No, Simone!" Nestaja cut her off.

"Okay, but I'm telling you, it works. Why you think I don't have problems from my ex anymore? I put a spell on that ass! Now I get my child support on time, he do what I want him to do. When I call, he stops what he is doing to do what I say with no back talk."

"Simone, that's witchcraft," Nestaja said.

"No, it's not. Only black magic is witchcraft. There's some you can do without using black magic."

"Okay, now I'm convinced you are crazy. I'm not voodooing my baby daddy." "It's not voodoo, it's more like a——"

"Oh, Simone, I got to go, my other line is beeping. I'll call you later," Nestaja said, cutting Simone off. "Hello?" she answered.

"May I speak to Natasha?"

Ghetto Diva

Now who is this with this fucked-up sounding voice getting my name all screwed up,

Nestaja thought. "Who's calling?"

"Is this Natasha?" the caller asked. "No, but this is Nestaja. Who this?"

"Don't worry about who I am. I know everything about you, and bitch, you better stay away from my husband."

"Well, sweetie, how am I going to know who to fuck tonight if you don't tell me who your husband is?" Nestaja sarcastically replied.

"Fuck you! Just stay away from my husband!"

Click! The caller hung up. Nestaja looked at the caller ID, but it read unknown caller. It really didn't faze Nestaja. Insecure females called her often, but it didn't bother her at all. It just let her know her game was always tighter than the person she was dealing with. She giggled and set the phone down.

It was still very early in the morning, so she decided to lay back down for a few hours.

As soon as she began to dose off, the doorbell rang.

"Who the hell is playing on my damn doorbell!" she yelled.

"Hey, sis, open the door. It's your bro."

"What the hell are you doing up and out this early in the morning?" she said as she opened the door.

"Hey, sis!" he said in a low tone.

"What's going on, bro? Why you look like you just came from a two year vacation with all this luggage?" Nestaja asked.

"I left my baby momma. I couldn't do it no more. I love my baby girl and all, but I hate her mama. I haven't been able to trust that bitch since she put me in jail. I tried for my daughter's sake, but I can't do it."

"About time you left that shady broad! I never liked her to begin with. I was just cordial with her for my niece's sake. She knows I can't stand her, and I wish she would even think about coming over here with all that drama! Busting windows out and messing up cars... I don't play those type of games. I'll beat the dust off her dusty ass."

"She's not going to come over here. I just need a place to rest my head until I get on my feet and get me some transportation and my own place."

"Oh, I'm not worried about her coming over here, and you can stay as long as you need to. I'm not trippin'. You can even drive my other car. Craz had it cleaned out real good after the incident, but since he got me a new whip, I haven't been driving it. As a matter of fact, let's pull it out the garage. You might want to rinse it off before you drive it. It's been sitting up for a little while."

"What's up with Craz, sis? I might need him to put me back in the game." "I'm sure he'll do it too. He's real cool and he don't mind helping people." "You not with my nigga S Man anymore?"

"Hell yeah, me and S Man are still together! As a matter of fact, I'm going to see him tomorrow. Craz is a financial blessing and someone to help pass time. You know can't nobody come between me and S Man."

"Sis, you crazy!"

He laughed as he headed to the kitchen. "What you got in here to eat? A nigga hungry."

"It's a little bit of everything in there. I'm going to make us some breakfast, but first let me wash up. Here is the key to the car. You can go put it in the driveway and wash it up a little bit. I'll be done with our breakfast when you're finished," Nestaja said, making her way to the shower.

Ding dong! Ding dong!

Why is everybody fucking with me this morning? Nestaja thought. "John, get the door!" she yelled from the bathroom.

"Who is it?" he yelled as he approached the door. "It's Jino," Reggie said, using his street name.

He opened the door. "Hey man, come on in and have a seat. Nestaja's in the bathroom."

When Reggie sat down, it appeared to him that someone was either coming or going on a vacation. John offered him something to drink and started to indulge in a conversation with him, not knowing what was up with him and Nestaja. He knew that his sister had gotten jumped, but he didn't know that Reggie had anything to do with it.

"What's been up with you, man?" Reggie asked.

"Not much, just take it a day at a time, trying keep my head above water. But what's been up with you?" John asked.

"You know my business, K & B tow? Well, I got seven tow trucks now and that's coming along pretty good. I just bought an 18-wheeler and a dump truck, and of course I still got them gallons, pounds and, pills on deck. If you know someone that is looking for it, I got it," Reggie replied.

"Okay, I'll keep that in mind," John responded as he headed out the door to rinse the car off.

Once he was outside, Reggie immediately rushed over to the luggage to see what was in it. He noticed there was some men's clothing inside, so he closed it back up and caught an instant attitude. *This bitch is moving her nigga in here*, he thought. *Nah, fuck that, I have to do something, because if he moves in, there will always be problems. Damn, I'm going to have to be nice to this bitch to get what I want. I'll also be plotting on how to get her ass back for all that extra bullshit she caused*, Reggie thought as he headed to the bathroom where Nestaja was taking her shower.

He walked in and stood there admiring her silhouette through the shower door before he made his presence known. "What's up, baby mama?" he said in a seductive tone.

Nestaja couldn't believe her ears. She snatched the shower door open, and there stood Reggie with a devious smile on his face.

"Get out of here, Reggie," she said in a surprised tone.

"Why? It ain't like I haven't seen you naked before," he responded.

Okay, Nestaja, girl, be nice so your plan can work, she thought. "Well, Reggie, it's not fair if you see me all wet and naked and you still got your clothes on," she said as she massaged her pierced clit.

"Is that an invite?" Reggie asked as he began to take off his clothes while thinking, *Stay focused. You're only doing this to plan your revenge.*

Reggie stepped into the shower with Nestaja and she teased him by letting the water fall from the shower on to her pierced tongue, moving it in a circular motion. He took the soap and towel and began to wash her back and the rest of her body until he had cleaned each and every part he was long awaiting to lick. He detached the showerhead and let the water stream on her, pleasing her pierced clit until she began to beg him to fuck her. She was turned on as the water glistened off his body.

Since she was so turned on, she decided to be the initiator, so she squatted down in front of him with him standing between her spread legs. She inserted his penis into her mouth and served him the way she knew he liked. She licked, sucked, took it deep in her throat, licked his balls until he reached his climax, and she swallowed every bit of it. She remembered that was a turn-on to him and kept him going.

He grabbed her and turned her face to the wall and entered her from behind. He took long deep strokes, went in deep he pulled her wet hair just as she liked it to be pulled. He then set her wet body on the edge of the tub and she leaned back with her hands touching the floor as he started to play with her piercing with his tongue. He licked her pussy just like she liked it to be licked. He fucked her with his tongue, and then he began to suck on her clit while he fingered her wet pussy. Then he put his dick inside of her and fucked her until she squirted everywhere. They both moaned and groaned the pleasant sounds of a well-reached climax.

After the sexual escapade, they played around in the shower for a while, cleaned each other up just like they used to, and then got dressed like nothing ever happened. Nestaja made breakfast as planned.

"Would you like some breakfast?" Nestaja asked Reggie.

"Nah, I'm good. I was just stopping by to see the kids. Where are they?" Reggie asked. "They're in Arizona with my momma," Nestaja answered.

"What you mean with your momma?" Reggie asked, aggravated.

"They're gonna be there for a while - at least until I get back on my feet. It's been real rough for me lately. My car is trippin', I have shut-off notices, but I'll be okay when I go back to the club. Katrina said business is pretty good there right now."

This bitch shouldn't have never got the kids in the first place. But I gotta maintain my composure to play this shit out right, Reggie thought. "Nestaja, you still bartending at the strip club?" Reggie questioned.

"Yes, I have to until I finish school. I plan on going back next semester."

Ghetto Diva

Remain calm, Reggie! Don't curse this bitch out. Just play it like everything is cool, act like everything she say is right, Reggie thought. "What happened to that so-called balling-ass nigga you had?" he questioned.

"Oh, Craz! I'm cool on him. I haven't really fucked with him since me and you went to jail."

"Yeah, right!"

"For real!" Nestaja assured him as she looked deep into Reggie's eyes. She knew he would get weak looking into her light browns.

"So, who you been fucking with?" Reggie asked. "Nobody. I'm focused on getting my shit together." "Well, I think we should – "

He was interrupted by John coming through the door. "There's a delivery truck outside looking for you. They said something about furniture," John said.

"Oh, um, that's my couch that my mom ordered for me. She was out here and spilled red soda on my other one and insisted on replacing it," she lied.

"What's wrong with your car?" Reggie asked.

"I don't know, but it cuts off a lot, and my check engine light stays on," she lied again. "Well, I don't want you getting stuck in traffic, so I'm going to bring you that lil Toyota

bucket I have. It's a year old, but it runs good. Someone owed me some money, but they gave me the car instead. Everything is in my name so it's mine, but I'm giving it to you, so make sure you change everything to your name."

"Okay, thank you!" Nestaja responded.

"Don't say I ain't never done nothing for you," he added.

"Oh, you did a whole lot for me in the shower," Nestaja said as she walked outside to greet the delivery guy.

"Ms. Simmons, we have your couch, fresh from Europe." "Oh, thanks. Can you place it right over there please?"

"Well, I'm leaving, but I'll bring the car in about an hour. Now don't mess the car up, Nestaja. I been driving it for about six months, and a few people know that I been pushing a silver lil bucket, so stay out of the projects. You know I got a few enemies over there, and they know that car. I heard them niggas put some hidden cameras up over there, so whatever you do, don't go over there in this car."

"Okay, but I don't hang out in the projects anyway."

"I'll be back with the car in a little bit," Reggie said as he jumped in his car and drove off.

Nestaja ran inside, grabbed her keys to her new car that was parked on the street, and told John to jump in the other car and follow her. She drove to Carson to her friend Mila's house.

Mila and Nestaja were not only godsisters, but they were also partners in crime. When those two were seen together, no one would dare try anything because they knew there would be some consequences and repercussions. Nestaja got out and rang the doorbell.

Mila's sister LeLe answered, happy to see Nestaja since they didn't see each other that often. But they talked all the time and were there for each other when they needed to be.

"Hey, girl!" LeLe greeted her with a hug. "Hey LeLe! Nestaja responded.

"How's Asia?"

"She's fine!"

"Tell that heffa to call me. It would be nice for us to all hang out sometime." "I know, we're long overdue."

"You too, Nestaja. You just don't come around anymore. We used to hang out, but now we hardly ever see each other."

"I know, LeLe. Once I shake this little dilemma I walked into, I'll be back around." "You're looking for Mila?" LeLe asked.

"Yeah, is she here?"

"No, she went to Mississippi to visit for a week. What's up?"

"I need to park my car in the garage for a while," Nestaja answered. "Why would you want to park that nice-ass car?" LeLe asked.

"I don't want Reggie to know I got it," Nestaja answered.

"Oh, go ahead. Here's the extra opener just in case you need to get it and we're not here."

"Okay, thanks LeLe. Tell Mila to call me as soon as she gets back."

"Okay, I will, see you later," LeLe said as Nestaja walked away and got in the car with her brother John.

As they drove home, Nestaja laced him on everything that was going on and told him not to deal with Reggie no matter what he offered him, because she had a plan that was going to take him and his whole entourage down. When Nestaja informed her brother of the incident that happened which had put her in jail and about her getting jumped, he was ready to tear Reggie a new asshole. But as always, Nestaja told him not to get involved and to let her handle it.

Chapter 13

After Reggie dropped the bucket off to Nestaja, she changed into something comfortable, since she knew she was meeting with the girls over at Akira's house in a few hours. After she changed clothes, she got in the bucket and opened the glove compartment. There was a camera, a set of keys, a screwdriver, and a letter. She opened it and it read: *What's up, Jino. I was sitting her thinking about you, and I hope all is well with you. We did get a chance to hook up with your baby mama and she should be down for a while - that's if she's able to even get back up again. I checked all your traps and everything is cool. I'll be so glad when you get out. I miss riding your dick, and drinking your cum. Well, I'll be up there to see you tomorrow, just wanted to let you know you're being thought of.*

Yours truly, Tina

She took the camera to 1-hour photo to get the pictures developed and put the letter in her purse. She drove to the liquor store and brought two bottles of Peach Ciroc. She wasn't a drinker, but Craz turned her on to the drink once when they were hanging out. Nestaja liked it, and ever since, either that or a glass of wine had been her drink of choice whenever she did decide to indulge. She looked at her iced-out designer watch that Craz had bought her and it was only 7:45. Looking at the watch and buying the drink made her think of Craz, so she decided to give him a call.

"What's up, sexy?" he answered.

"Hey baby, I miss you!" she responded.

"I know, baby, I been working all these long hours, and I don't have an off day until Sunday, so I'm going to leave Sunday open just for you," Craz replied.

Ghetto Diva

She knew that wouldn't work since she was going to see S Man on Sunday, and she wasn't going to let anything stop her from doing so. "Baby, I have some important business to take care of and I won't be available until Monday evening."

"Okay, that's cool, babe, we'll hook up Monday around eight. I'm going to leave work early," he stated.

"Okay, that's cool, I'll see you Monday night. Talk to you then," she responded.

Still with a little time on her hands, she decided to go to her neighborhood to see what was happening on the block. She pulled up on 97th and parked under a tree. Everyone was out and the block was crackin'. Nestaja hadn't been to the hood in a while so she was anxious to kick it with her loved ones.

She got out of the car, and as soon as she headed across the street, she noticed the helicopter hovering over the block. Before she could ask what was going on, Task hit the block like fruit flies on an old banana. She didn't want any problems with the law, so she crept back to the car and managed to drive off without being noticed.

An hour had passed, so she went back to the 1-hour photo to get the pictures. She looked through them, and they were pictures of two girls having sex with each other, posing for the camera and showing their goods. She took a good look at the pictures and noticed it was indeed one of the girls that jumped her. She sat there for a while in a rage, looking at the pictures. She put them in her purse and drove off. As she hit the corner, her cell phone rang.

"Hello?" she answered.

"Didn't I tell you to stop calling my husband?" the unknown caller with the raspy voice yelled.

"Well, maybe if you tell me who your husband is, I can tell you how good or bad his dick is," Nestaja replied.

"Fuck you, Natasha, don't let me catch you slippin'."

"Well, I'm slippin' down Avalon and Century in a silver bucket. Come see me," Nestaja responded.

"Natasha, you don't want to see me," the raspy-voiced caller said.

"No, bitch, you must wanna see me, because you keep calling my phone. Learn how to say my name, then holla at me," Nestaja demanded as she hung up the phone, wondering, *Who is this person that keeps calling my phone from a blocked number about a nigga? Well, whoever it is, she's a punk bitch because she won't make herself known. Fuck it, it is what it is.* Looking at her watch she saw that she still had some time to kill, so she decided to go to grab something to eat from Roscoe's. She had planned on having a few drinks, but not too many, because she knew she had to get up at 4:30 a.m. to be there by 9:00 a.m. to get her full six-hour visit with S Man.

When she pulled in the parking lot, the parking lot attendant approached her car and told her she needed to park on the street.

"I'll just pull in one of those two parking spots since I'm just ordering take out," Nestaja said.

"No, you're not. You're going to park on the street like I told you to," the attendant stated.

"Well, I'm just getting take out, I'm not staying, and those two spots are empty. Are you holding them for someone?"

"Bitch, it don't matter if I'm holding them for someone, I said park on the street."

"Hold up! You don't have to get at me like I'm a little girl. There's a way to talk to people to get the response you want."

"Well, this is my parking lot, and what I say goes," he said in a very angry tone.

"Cuz, you got me way fucked up. I don't give a fuck whose parking lot this is. You gon' give me my respect," Nestaja demanded as she got out of the car, walking up on the guard.

"Bitch, you need to get yo' yellow ass back in that car before you get yourself fucked up," he said as he prepared himself for whatever she was about to give him.

"Check this out, Otis!" she said as she grabbed his name badge. "I'll shoot your dick through your asshole if you don't apologize to me right now!" she informed him as she touched the front of his pants with her pistol.

"Well, bitch, do it!"

"Hey, Otis, what's going on over there?" a familiar voice yelled. "Man, that's a female, what are you doing?" he said as he walked up, pushing Otis away from her.

"Aww, man, I'm sorry, I'm having a bad day."

"That's your problem. You always starting something, and it's always with females.

You're not getting away with this shit today. You always putting your foot in your mouth," he stated while pushing Otis to the ground. He walked over to Nestaja to see if she was okay.

"You cool, lil mama?" he asked.

"Yeah, but he needs to learn how to talk to people," Nestaja said as she got back in her car.

"Yeah, dude don't have no chill. I'm always seeing him get into it with females, but always let these niggas get a pass. You go ahead and park where you want to and enjoy your meal."

"Thank you!"

She parked her car in the empty spot and headed inside to place her order. "How may I help you?" the waitress asked.

"Yes, I would like to place an order to go," Nestaja replied. "Okay, what are you having today?"

"I'll have the number 9 with a Lisa's Delight."

"Okay, that will take about 15-20 minutes. Your order number is 76. Can you have a seat please? Someone will call your number when it's ready."

"Okay, thanks!" she responded.

As she went to sit down she heard someone yelling, "DENYSE!"

She didn't pay it any mind because no one called her by her middle name except her older aunties.

"DENYSE!" she heard someone yell again.

She looked around and there were her aunties Carolyn Jean, Connie, her Uncle Alvin, and her godmother Ruby having dinner.

"Hey! What y'all doing in here?" Nestaja asked as she greeted them all. "Oh, we're just grabbing a bite to eat," Carolyn Jean answered.

"Where are you on your way to, missy?" Rudy asked.

"I'm going over Akira's house. We're having one of our little get togethers and a few drinks," Nestaja answered.

"Yeah, we know how those get togethers can end up," Alvin added, which caused everyone to burst out into laughter.

"Yeah, y'all get drunk and want to beat up everybody in L.A.," Connie said. "We're getting to old for all that. We're just getting together to have a few drinks."

"Since when did you start drinking?" One asked. "I indulge every now and then," she responded.

"We heard what happened with you and them kids' daddy. You know you don't have to put up with him and all that drama he brings you. I personally like that new guy with that truck on them big ole nice rims. He treats you and them kids well, and he's very respectful," Ruby mentioned.

"And he can cook his behind off. He makes the best macaroni and cheese," Connie added "Yeah, he's cool, but everything that shine ain't always gold," Nestaja replied.

"Number 76, your order is ready!"

"Well, okay, enjoy the rest of y'all night. Let me get my food and get outta here." "Now don't go getting in any trouble, girl," Carolyn Jean said.

"I'm not!" she replied.

She paid for her food and headed to Akira's house.

Chapter 14

A pleasant tropical aroma filled the room while Akira danced around to the sounds of Kendrick Lamar as she tidied up the house before the girls got there. She made sure all the nice expensive things she had gotten from Kenneth were in plain view. When she heard the chimes of her doorbell, she excitedly skipped over to answer it.

"What it do!" Asia greeted as she walked into Akira's house. "Oh, nothing!" Akira responded with a big smile on her face. "Why you smiling so hard?" Asia questioned.

"No reason!" Akira sang.

"Whatever, bitch. You are smiling too hard for it to be nothing!"

"I went to Ensenada with Kenneth for a few days. We just got back a few hours ago." "You chillin' with the enemy like it's the thing to do. Fuck the po-po's! I hope you got

something out of it!" Asia stated.

"Why I got to get something out of it? Why I couldn't just go to have some fun? Oops!" Akira said as she purposely dropped her large designer bag on the floor. "Oh no, all of my stuff fell out." She purposely bent over, letting her new diamond-studded necklace dangle from her neck.

"Okay, Akira, I see you're smart enough to not fuck for free or on IOU's like a lot of these hoes," Asia commented while helping her pick up a few items and some money from the floor. "You sure you weren't out there stripping? Or was he pimping you?" Asia joked.

"Nope, but I will say this. All cops ain't good cops, and I got one of the naughtiest ones there is," Akira announced as she walked over to answer the front door.

"Hey, biiotch!" Nestaja entered with a bottle of liquor in each hand. "What? Ms. Miss Innocent got bottles?" Akira questioned.

"Last time I checked, you didn't drink," Asia added. "I can when I want to, and tonight I want to."

"Just don't start blowing. I need your pee to stay clean so we can pass these drug tests," Asia commented while she reached over and met Akira's hand halfway, making a high five in agreement.

But Nestaja didn't pay them any mind. She continued on to the kitchen to pour herself a drink.

"Damn, what's up with her?" Asia asked Akira.

"I don't know, but a few drinks from time to time might be just what her uptight ass needs," Akira responded.

"Don't let Nestaja fool you. I know when she be at the club mixing them drinks, she be hooking herself up a few," Asia replied.

"You think so?"

"Hell yeah! You can't work in a strip club, talk shit like she do, flirt and get big tips like she do and be sober," Asia pointed out.

"Hum, I didn't think about that."

"I hear y'all hoes talking about me." Nestaja walked in on their conversation just as Netra and Monique walked through the door.

They sat down and Nestaja got straight to the point. "Netra, what's up with them bitches that jumped me?"

"I know all four of 'em. But the main one is Vickie. She used to live across the hall from me. Them bitches got evicted because the police was always at their house, so Section 8 put them out. Before they got put out, the police kicked the door in and found some dope and guns and took a few of them to jail, but Vickie bailed out. Her ass was over there struggling, trying to get what she could before the Marshals put the lock on the door. They probably moved back to the projects. They just some low budget ratchet-ass broads, with no job, and they hustle for cheap. They used to run for your baby daddy. I heard Vickie's sister Wanda got him for some money, and that is how they bailed out of jail. He went to the projects looking for them bitches and ended up in a shootout with they brother, Big Bayru. He's the shot caller and the money man over there. From weed to speed. He got the projects on lock."

"What he look like?" Akira asked.

"He cool. Y'all probably seen him around. He push a big red truck on some big rims or a red convertible luxury coupe. He owns the car wash on Central. I heard him and your baby daddy was cool until they had that little shootout. But the other two are they homegirls, April and Tina. Tina and Vickie were the ones that stabbed you; April and Wanda are the two fighters. I got an earful after they came back because they were pumped up and talking about who did what. After listening to them talk and putting two and two together, I figured it all out. Then I

found out you were in the hospital. So now it's time for you to get them bitches back," Netra stated.

"One of them bitches fuck with Reggie," Nestaja said. "Yeah, I think Tina, she's the only decent one."

"It don't matter. I'm gonna get all them bitches."

The front door flew opened and in walked a vibrant, turnt up Katrina.

"Heyyy, I'm late, but I hope y'all got blunts, because I got that good," Katrina announced, waving a large Ziploc bag of medical marijuana.

"Katrina, yo' ass always late."

"Akira, I know you ain't talking. Yo' ass would have been late too if we wasn't at your house," Nestaja added.

"Where is Crystal?" Katrina questioned.

"Her and Michael going through it again, so y'all already know she is going to be MIA for some months."

Katrina opened the bag, allowing the strong aroma of the medical marijuana to fill the room.

"Damn, Katrina, whose dick did you suck to get that?" Asia asked.

"I been a good bitch since I left DJ. Me and my new nigga Deshon have been kicking it tough, and I don't want to mess that up. He knows too many niggas in these streets. I don't want to get caught up in my bullshit," Katrina answered.

"I feel you. I'm going to go see S Man tomorrow, and I want to know what his intentions are when he come home, because we're not getting younger," Nestaja added.

"What are you going to do about Craz?" Akira questioned as she poured a second round. "I don't know. He's cool and I care about him, but I don't love him."

"Well, I know you love what he do for you," Katrina commented. "Yeah, girl, that nigga loves you," Akira added.

"I think he is just infatuated with my hood and freaky ways. I found out about four or five bitches that he fucks with on a regular when he left his phone at my house, and I checked his messages, so I know what he is all about. I'm just glad that I found out before I did fall in love with him. This is a pattern for him. He's a charmer with a big dick and a talented tongue. On top of all that, we have been seeing each other for about two years now and I haven't met any of his kids or family members. I guess it is what it is. What bitch that's on her game wouldn't fall for a sexy gangsta with a bomb-ass job and a few good side hustles?"

"Damn, you do have a point," Asia added.

"Now don't get me wrong, Craz is my dude and I appreciate all the things he do, but I know his charming ways is going to cause him to stray away. If I don't brace myself, I'll be the one getting hurt. So I've already prepared myself for it, because I know it's coming real soon."

"What you mean?" Katrina asked.

"I can feel something ain't right. I can't put my finger on it, but it'll all come out." "Well, Kenneth and me are real cool, but he likes me to strap up and fuck him in the ass,"

Akira said.

"Ugggh, he is gay! That is so gross!" Asia responded.

"No, I guess he's bi, cuz he does have a wife and kids. His wife teaches law enforcement classes at the community college - that's where they met. He goes up there frequently to speak with the students, and he patrols the area. I told him I don't want him to fuck me unless he leaves his wife, and I know he's not going to do that because he loves her a lot. I know because he always talks about her. She just won't get freaky with him, so that was basically my excuse to not give him my cookie. I'm just doing whatever he wants me to do to keep them dollars and gifts coming in," Akira bragged.

"Damn, bitch, you got some shit on him. If you can get pictures of that and post it somewhere, the whole police force will be humiliated."

"I know, and so does he. That's why he is going to do whatever I need him to do. He's real cool. He is just scared to death of cats," Akira responded while giving the girls their third round of drinks.

"Imagine that, he scared of a little pussy cat," Monique said, causing the girls to burst into laughter.

"I forgot to tell y'all, Gina is coming home next week. Let's put together a party for her," Katrina mentioned.

"Oh, that's what's up! I miss my lil cousin. It's been hot, so let's do a pool party," Nestaja suggested.

"We're not having a pool party at my house!" Asia threw out there. "Mine either," Katrina added.

"I'm sure we can do it at my auntie's house. She'll be happy to let the family come over and see that nice-ass house she keep bragging about. We'll just give her the money and tell her what we want and let her do all the work," Asia suggested.

"We can all help with the cooking," Akira added.

"I'll bring the fire." Katrina picked up the bag of weed, waving it around.

"I got the drinks," Nestaja added.

"I ain't doing nothing. I spent about six racks on the bitch at the mall today." "But Asia, we need you on the grill."

"No! I don't want my clothes smelling like hickory all day. Have somebody else do it," Asia responded.

"I'll reach out to everybody and let them know what's up." Nestaja stood up and took her drink to the neck.

"Damn, Nestaja, you sure have been drinking a lot tonight," Akira pointed out. "This drink is bomb, and it's going to help me sleep tonight."

"Whatever, bitch, you know you be throwing them back all night when you are bartending at the feline lounge," Asia joked as she hit the blunt and passed it.

"Oh, Nestaja, when are you coming back to work anyway? The club has been turned up and the money been rollin' in," Katrina informed her.

"I'll be back this Thursday."

"A lot of people have been asking about you, so you know you're missing money." Katrina took a long hard pull on the blunt before she advised, "Friday is my last night. I'm giving up the pole."

"Why? You make good money there," Monique asked.

"I never planned on dancing the rest of my life. It was just temporary to keep some money in my pockets. Now that I'm with Deshon, he's going to be the breadwinner. I'm going to stay home and take care of the house and kids."

"This nigga has successfully turned a hoe into a housewife. I didn't think it could be done. I'm happy for you, bitch," Nestaja commented.

"Well, who you think I learned from? You're the oldest," Katrina shot back. "But forget all that. What are we going to do about them project bitches?"

"I need to get some information on all of them. I'm going to start pushing through their lil spots." Nestaja answered.

"Be careful going over there. They've been at war knocking down niggas and bitches daily," Asia advised.

"I need to think this out. I can't get caught up in somebody else bullshit." Nestaja quickly went into deep thought of how she could execute her plan as she slowly sipped the last little bit of her drink.

"Akira, tell bitch boy to get as much information on them that he can," Asia joked, which caused everyone to burst out into laughter.

"I'm out. I have to get up in a few hours to go see S Man," Nestaja said as she stumbled to the door.

"Bitch, you're too tipsy to drive home. I'll take you," Asia demanded. "What about my car?" Nestaja asked.

"I can follow Asia to your house, and she can just drop me back off in the hood," Akira suggested.

"Let's go. I need some rest before I go see my nigga."

"Wait, I got to pee first," Asia said as she jumped up and ran to the bathroom.

"Every time this bitch drink, she gotta pee about nine times before we walk out the door and seven more before we arrive at our destination," Katrina joked.

"We out too. Me and Monique don't see y'all often, but we'll be in touch," Netra said as she and Monique headed out the door.

Chapter 15

Beep, beep, beep, beep!

*D*amn, *its 4:30 already?* Nestaja thought as she rolled out of bed. She went into the bathroom, washed her face, brushed her pretty whites, and ran herself some hot bath water. She went to her closet to pick out something to wear. She knew she couldn't wear anything too revealing, because the guards would sometimes be hating and would send her to change or she wouldn't get a visit. She looked over the visiting guidelines that S Man sent her to make sure she didn't wear what they didn't allow. Even though she had become cool with most of the guards from going up there to visit, she still didn't want to take a chance.

To reassure herself, she went over the visiting guideline restrictions again: no clothing which in any combination of shades or types of material/fabric resembles California State-issued inmate clothing, blue denim or chambray shirts and blue denim pants. No law enforcement or military-type forest green or camouflage patterned articles of clothing, including rain gear. No hats, wigs, or hairpieces (except with prior written approval of the Visiting Sergeant). No clothing that exposes the breast/chest area, genital area, or buttocks. No dresses, skirts, pants, or shorts exposing more than two inches above the knee, including slits, sheer, or transparent garments. No strapless or "spaghetti" straps. No clothing exposing the midriff area. No clothing or accessories displaying obscene or offensive language or drawings. Brassieres with metal under wires or any other detectable metal are not permitted.

Damn, what can I wear? she thought as she grabbed her cute lime green and yellow designer tunic dress with some matching sandals and a clutch. She decided to not wear any panties. The opportunity might present itself, and S Man might want to play around in his playpen. She also grabbed her fitted sweat suit with matching tennis shoes, just in case they hated on her with the dress. She got in the tub, took a good wash-up, got out, lotioned her body, and sprayed a little perfume on. She got dressed and sprayed a little more perfume on her, because she knew that was S Man's favorite. She hooked up her hair, makeup, and accessories, looked at the clock, and it was 5:24 a.m. She was right on time. She grabbed her clutch, her bag of extra clothes, and her Ziploc bag of quarters, which they allowed visitors to bring in so they could purchase items from the vending machines. Then she rushed out the front door, anxious to see her sweetie.

Once she arrived on the campgrounds, she put her clutch purse in the trunk along with her bag of extra clothes and headed to the visiting building, praying she didn't have to change. She went in the bathroom and looked herself over to make sure everything was in top-notch condition after that three-hour drive. She stood in line to go through all the extras they sent the visitors through. After twenty minutes, her turn came up to turn in her visitor's pass and go through the metal detectors.

"Please take your shoes off and place them on the conveyor belt," the guard stated. "And walk on this dirty floor with my bare feet?" Nestaja asked.

"Girl, yeah, that's a new thing they just started a few weeks ago," the girl behind her told her.

"Well, that's stupid! I know I haven't been up here in a few months, but damn, how much more done changed?" Nestaja asked.

"I know, I ain't seen you up here in a while, but a whole lot done changed," the girl replied.

"Yeah, I been busy tryna get thangs right for when my dude come home," Nestaja responded.

"I feel you. My man come home next month, and I know I'm not ready. I'ma be glad, but I know shit 'bout ta change," the girl said.

"How long he been locked up?"

"Girl, five years, and I been visitin' his ass faithfully. I used to see you up here, but we neva got a chance to meet. My name's Ebony," she said as she stuck her hand out to shake Nestaja's.

"Hi, I'm Nestaja."

"Oh, okay, nice to finally meet you," Ebony said as she and Nestaja sat on a concrete bench, putting their shoes back on.

"How much more time yo' man got?" Ebony asked. "He real short."

"Do y'all have kids together?"

Damn, dis bitch nosy, Nestaja thought. "No, but we been together off and on since our teenage years."

"Well, me and Patrick have four kids. We been together for seven years now. We only had one when he first got locked up. Now we got four."

"Damn, how y'all manage to do that?" Nestaja asked as she got up, heading to the visiting room with Ebony walking next to her.

"Where there's a will, there's a way." Ebony giggled.

"I ain't mad at cha, do ya thang," Nestaja responded.

As they got closer to the visiting room, Nestaja noticed a male figure that resembled S Man. She wasn't sure because she could only see the back of this person sitting next to a female, so she started to walk faster and harder.

"Girl, you alright?" Ebony asked, running along the side of her.

"I'm not sure just yet," Nestaja replied. As she got closer, she noticed it was S Man sitting in the visiting room with a female. "This nigga got a bitch up here?" she mumbled.

"I've seen that girl maybe three or four times up here wit' him. I didn't wanna say anything cuz I didn't wanna seem messy."

"You know her name?" Nestaja asked.

"No, I neva met her, I just seen her a couple of times on a visit with him."

Before I approach him, let me make sure it's not a family member, Nestaja thought as she walked over to make her presence known. "Hey, daddy!" she said as she stood in front of him, looking at his unknown visitor.

"Oh, ummm, what's up, Nestaja?" he said as he stood up and

greeted her with a hug and kiss.

"Baby, who's she?" Nestaja questioned. "Oh, um, this is, um, Shay. Shay, this is—"

"I'm his girl, Nestaja," she said, cutting him off as she stuck her hand out to give Shay a firm handshake.

"His girl?" Shay asked, looking at S Man. "Um, yeah, this my girl, Shay."

"You ain't mentioned nothing about a girlfriend, S Man. And don't think I'm leavin'. I'm stayin' right her for the rest of my visit, cuz I didn't drive all the way out here for nothin'."

"Oh, is that what you think?" Nestaja said as she sat right in front of them on the edge of the bench, waiting on a response from S Man.

"Shay, this my girl, she gon' always come first, so you gotta bounce."

"What you mean, I gotta bounce? I been writing, putting money on yo' books, taking chances puttin' shit in my pussy, bringin' it up here, running up my phone bill, sendin' yo' ass packages in everybody's name but yours, and you gon' tell me I need to bounce, S Man?"

"Check this out. I been with Nestaja for damn near twenty years. This my girl. I hate you found out this way, but it is what it is. So you need to leave so I can kick it with my girl. I'm askin' you nicely. Don't make me show you."

"Well, I guess you gon' have to show me 'cause I ain't goin' nowhere," she replied as she leaned back on the bench.

"Well, bitch, I don't know who you gon' visit, but it won't be my nigga," Nestaja added as she squeezed in between the two, causing Shay to fall off the bench.

"I'm still not goin' nowhere."

"Aye, check this out, homegirl, if you make a scene and my nigga get caught up behind yo' bullshit, ain't nobody gon' get a visit, cuz I'ma give 'em a reason to lock this whole muthafucka down," Nestaja said through clenched teeth while making it appear as if she was helping her up, but she was really twisting her arm with a firm aggressive grip and threatening her.

"Fuck you, S Man!" Shay shouted as got up and headed toward

the gate. "What the fuck was that all about?" Nestaja angrily asked.

"Come on, baby, don't start this, please."

"What the fuck you mean don't start? This shit was started before I got here. Nigga, I call myself surprising you, but I'm the one that got surprised."

"Baby, listen, she ain't nothin'. Just a bitch my celly know, and I used her as a mule to produce the goodies that I need."

"Ain't that what I'm here for?"

"Yeah, if push came to shove. But I stay on top of my shit, so it don't get to that point. As long as I got a bitch in my corner that's willing to step up and take the fall, your position will remain safeguarded."

"Do you love her?"

"Hell nah! It ain't nothing like that, Staja, fuck her! She don't mean shit to me."

Now is the time to put all my hoe cards on the table, Nestaja thought. "You know what? I ain't gonna' trip, 'cause my closet ain't that clean either," she admitted.

"What the fuck you mean by that?"

"I been dealing with somebody too, and he been keeping me financially blessed. He means nothing to me. He was just somebody to help me through hard times."

"Did you give the nigga my pussy?" "Don't ask me that."

"Fuck that, that's my shit! I was the first one to bust that muthafucka open. It's fucked up you went out and had a baby by that nigga Jino. I hope you ain't out there bein' a hoe, makin' a nigga look bad?"

"S Man! I'm not answering no crazy-ass questions. I just want to make it right between us from this point on. I'm tired of living in L.A. I want a change. Both of our hoods are hot as hell, the city is full of haters, and I don't like living in L.A. no more."

"So, you tellin' me you gonna lay down on a nigga?"

"No, baby, I'm saying I want us to move on with our lives and do bigger and better things as a family. We're not gettin' younger, and I know we made mistakes, but look at us. We're still together," she said while looking into his eyes so he could feel her sincerity.

"I been kinda feelin' the same way lately. A nigga do need to settle down, cuz it ain't nothin' in the streets but trouble that will have a nigga back in this muthafucka or dead. I'm missin' out on too much bein' in here." He ran his fingers through her hair.

"Let's move to Arizona," Nestaja suggested. "Arizona? Baby, it's hot as hell out there."

"It's only hot 3-4 months out the year, and it's only 4 ½ to 5 hours from L.A. if we gotta go back for an emergency. The cost of living is unbelievably cheap. The price I'm paying for that raggedy-ass house on the east side, we could be buying a house and living large in Arizona. Baby, think about it, it's for our kids, our future, and us."

"So, what about this nigga you been fucking with?"

"Okay, I'ma keep it real with you, he cool and I was feeling him. But when I realized what he was all about, my feelings changed. He the type that like to be needed and praised for what he do. He got about five females that he takes care of, and that ain't including his nine kids and eight baby mommas. He's only around to pacify the moment and help me keep your locker full and packages coming."

"Well, you better enjoy the moment for now and be ready to shut it down when I come home. I'm tellin' you this because I need to hold onto Shay for a few more months. The bitch send me money by the thousands. But from now on, I'ma have her send the money to my momma and you go get it and put it towards our house in Arizona, and you need to do the same with the money you get from that nigga. You hear me?"

"Yes, I hear you, babe!" Nestaja replied.

"I ain't got a whole lot of time like muthafuckas think I do. I'm real short to come home." "When you getting out?" Nestaja asked.

"You'll be comin' to get me sooner than you think, nigga, so tighten up your shit so we can bounce and do us, then come back and stunt on these haters."

"Okay!" Nestaja said as she leaned over and kissed him on the cheek. "Baby, I miss you so much! I'ma be so glad when this shit is over," she added as she watched a guard approach them, looking a little suspicious. As the guard got closer, he kicked a balled-up brown paper bag toward them.

"Pick that up and hand it to me," S Man instructed.

Nestaja picked it up and gave it to him. He opened it and there was a key with a number #6 on it, and "45" was marked on the bag.

"See that building right there to your left by the bathroom?" "Yes!" she answered.

"That's where we're going. But first go in the bathroom wait for minute, then creep out and slide in door #6. I'ma be in there waitin' on you."

Nestaja followed his instructions. When she got in the ladies room, she looked herself over, then crept out. Since door #6 was right next to the bathroom, she slid in without being noticed into what appeared to be a storage room with a mattress in it. Just as promised, S Man was right there. He locked the door with the key and began kissing her passionately while walking her backwards. He grabbed her by her hair, saying with aggression, "Bitch, gimme my pussy!"

She was definitely turned on by his aggression. She took her shoes off and lifted her dress, exposing her pretty, clean-shaven pussy. He got a tighter grip on her hair and slammed her into the wall, kissing her while he finger-fucked her. Once she managed to get her dress off, she began to undress him. By the time they were undressed, they were both hot and horny.

Nestaja leaned back on the mattress and opened her legs, exposing her pussy. She put her finger in her mouth, then used it to rub her clit while admiring his sexy chocolate, muscular body. He stood back and enjoyed the sight for a few seconds.

Neither of them could take it anymore so she got up, roughly laid him on the mattress, and straddled his dick, riding like she was on an electric bull. He moaned and groaned while he exploded inside of her. She got off his dick and cleaned it with her mouth and tongue. He flipped her on her back and put her feet on his chest as he began to slowly deep-stroke her pussy with his 10 ½ inch dick, and she enjoyed each and every stroke. He took both her legs, put them on his shoulders, and worked on her spot for about ten minutes until she exploded.

The shaking, the wetness, and the thought of him making her

pussy squirt like that caused him to nut in her pussy again. His dick was still hard and her pussy was dripping wet. He leaned her over a table and held on to her shoulders while beating it up from the back until he came in her again. With that last nut, there was a knock on the door, which meant time was up. He told her to go to the bathroom and wash up and then meet him back at the bench. She crept to the ladies room, and in her attempt to clean, up she rubbed on her pussy a little bit, still horny for S Man's dick. But she had to calm herself down since she knew that she wouldn't be able to get anymore anytime soon. She washed up and walked back over to the bench.

"Damn, babe, you my thug bitch. I love that about you. You ain't no shy bitch, no corny bitch, no homie bitch. You can pull it off at a red-carpet event and you can Crip walk down the blue carpet at a hood function. My bitch wit' the business - you know how to hustle, you got that sexiness, book smarts, that ghetto spunk, that toughness, street savvy, and the cold part about it. Ya nigga know you. I know you better than any nigga or bitch on these streets, 'cause I made you the bitch you are today. A nigga need all those elements in a woman. It'll take ten bitches to be one of you. Daddy miss his bitch," he said as he got a quick sneak peek of her jewels as she sat down. "Baby, what's wrong?" he asked.

"Do you get down like that all the time?" she questioned.

"I just expressed some real hood love to you and that's your reply? And no, Staja, I had it set up for when my boy that work in the visiting room sees you to make it happen. They know who you are, and they know you my wifey."

"You never took Shay back there?"

"I took her back there for a five minute fuck, and I made her bring condoms. It was just somethin' I did to release the build-up. But I saved my forty-five minutes for you. I'm keeping it real with you cuz I love you and I'm lookin' forward to spendin' my future with you."

Although she was hurt and pissed off, what could she say with all the fucking she had been doing? "We finna bump this shit way down with the sex outside our relationship from this point on," she stated.

"You know I'm cool with that, 'cause I hate that you gave my pussy away. Nobody shoulda never been in that but me. So whatever went on before today, we gon' leave it behind us. I'm with you! You my bitch. I don't care about shit else out there but you and our kids," he said as he lifted her head up by her chin with his finger. "We always had a joyous time with each other. No matter what I did, you stood strong through it all. Then when we separated, you went your way and I went mine. You did some thangs you shouldn't have done and I did some thangs I shouldn't have done. The worst part was we was away from each other. Are you listenin' to me?" he asked, noticing she was in deep thought.

"Yes, I'm listening."

"Nestaja, has anybody come into your life that was better than me?" "Nope!"

"You feel I'm the one you should be with?" "Um-hmm, I sure do."

"I feel that way too." "You do?"

"Yeah, I feel that way."

"So, will you do me the honor of being my wife?"

"Awww, yes, you gon' make me cry! Yes, you know I will." "Will you love me to no end?"

"Yes, I will."

"You'll be every lady to me that I need?" "Everything and then some!"

"And never ever leave me?" "I ain't goin' nowhere."

"Nestaja, I promise to love you forever, cherish you, never disappoint you, always pick you up when you down, always be your best friend and a shoulder you can lean on. I'm yo' everythang. So Ms. Nestaja Denyse Simmons, would you be my wife?"

"Yes, I will, Sheldon Rasheed Gibson."

"Thank you! Don't you worry about nothin'. I got you. Our past is our past. I love everything that got your blood in it. I'm not the biological, but Jasmine and Josiah are my kids. I love them like I planted those seeds."

"They know you do, and they love you like you're their daddy. Mrs. Nestaja Gibson…I love how it sound. I love you, S Man."

"I love you too, Nestaja. I'ma make you happy 'til yo' eyes close.

Ghetto Diva

I promise I'ma stay true to you, I promise I'ma be sincere, you don't never have to worry. I got you! I'm not gon' settle for something less and do something stupid and leave you. Every move is gonna be calculated. You gon' get all the man outta me, I owe you that. I'm not gon' give us no extras, baby. I promise, even when I'm out doin' my thug thang, you gon' have that sense of security knowin' yo' husband ain't out fuckin' up. Them days are over. You got that?"

"Yes, I got it."

"So, you need to start cleanin' up house and gettin' my shit ready for me to come home, 'cause I don't want none of the shit you doin' comin' into our marriage."

"I got you, daddy."

"Damn, I love yo' yellow ass, girl! You my bitch. I knew when me and my brother met you and Asia in the sunny swap meet on Vermont back in the day I was gon' bust that lil pussy out, and I knew you was gon' be mine forever."

"You knew that back then?"

"Hell yeah, I knew!" he answered while stroking her neck with his finger.

The rest of the visit went perfect. She told him what was going on with Reggie and the kids and updated him on all the street activity. They talked, laughed, and joked for a few hours until it was time to end the visit. It was hard for her to say goodbye, but she did it, and she promised to do everything he expected her to do because she was definitely fed up with the way things were going in L.A. She hugged and kissed him and he told her not to get in any trouble, because sometimes it was best to walk away and leave certain situations up to God. They hugged again and went their separate ways.

When she got to her car, she checked her cell phone and it read eight missed calls and four new messages. She dialed her voicemail.

"Hey girl, this is Taj. My mom wants to meet with you before your court date at the end of the month. She pulled some strings for you, so give me a call, and we also need to set a time and place for our lunch date next week." Message deleted.

"Hey, beautiful, I'm looking forward to seeing you tomorrow, can't wait to taste that pussy." Message deleted.

"Hey, girl, this is Mila. LeLe told me you came through and dropped your car off, what's going on? Hit me later." Message deleted.

"Hey, bitch, daddy lettin' us take the yacht out today. I know you visitin' S Man. If you get this before 2:00, call me." Message deleted.

"Nestaja, this is Netra. I'm at Juiced by Nesha's hair salon, and one of them bitches that jumped you just came in here. The shop is crowded, so she's going to be here a while. Ya might wanna come through. It's 4:02, call me when you get this. 323-555-0021." Message saved.

She looked at her watch. *Good I have time*, she thought as she put her seatbelt on, preparing herself for the 3 ½ hour trip. She made a call to Nesha.

"Hey, Nesha, girl, this Nestaja. I got an extreme emergency. I need you to squeeze me and Simone in."

"Okay, come on. I plan on hanging out at the shop kinda late tonight anyway, so come on."

"Okay, I'll see you in a lil bit."

She scrolled through her contacts in her cell phone and called Simone. "Hello?"

"What's up, biotch!"

"Hey, Nestaja, what's up with you?"

"Nothing much, just came from seeing S Man." "Did you enjoy your visit?"

"Umm-hmmmm!"

"He must have played with your little bubble gum."
"Ummm-hmmmmm, but I didn't call to talk about that. I called to ask you about the juice."

"What juice?" Simone replied.

"You know what juice I'm talking about," Nestaja said. "Ooh, the juice!"

"What'cha you doin' right now?"

 "Nothing, why, what's up?"

"Let's go get our hair done. My treat," Nestaja offered.

"I could use a good wash and flat-iron. Okay, when you coming?"

Ghetto Diva

"I'll be there in about two hours."

"A'ight, see you when you get here," Simone said as she hung up.

Nestaja went through her messages again and got Netra's number and called her. "Hey Netra, I just got your message, what's up?"

"Yeah, that bitch April is up here."

"Well, I'm on my way. Be cool with her, and when I get there, follow my lead." "Okay, I'll see you when you get here."

Nestaja floored the lil bucket and made it to LA in 2 ½ hours. She picked up Simone, but didn't really tell her what was going on. Simone wasn't a hood girl like the rest, and she didn't want her to get scared and mess up her plan, so she just inquired about the juice and what went in it. Simone told her about the Belizean remedy and where she could find the ingredients. She then asked Nestaja what she needed it for.

"You know all those cats by my house? I want to get rid of them."

"Well, the murder juice will definitely get rid of them, and your baby daddy too if you want me to hook that up for you."

"Girl, you're crazy!"

"No, I'm serious! Nestaja, it's a known fact that the juice leaves no trace in the system. When someone drinks it, it deteriorates their insides in a matter of one to four months, and the autopsy comes back as if they died from natural causes. A lot of my people in Belize have gotten away with it without any suspicion at all."

"Girl, I'm not tryna kill Reggie. I don't like his ass, but at the same time, I don't want him dead or in jail. I might want him to suffer a little, but not to the point where it affects the kids."

"Well, if you change your mind, let me know, and like I told you before, I'll put a hex on his ass."

"Girl, you are crazy, for real."

They arrived at the salon and went in and sat down with Netra and April and immediately became a part of the conversation. Nestaja knew she wouldn't be remembered from the day she got jumped. She had her hair pulled back in a ponytail with a baseball cap and some sweats and it was dark, and from the time she spent in the hospital, she had lost a few pounds. So the girl sat there and talked with them for hours. She enjoyed herself so much she even hung out after Nesha was done with her hair.

They were there until 1:30 a.m. Their hair was all done and Nestaja was getting sleepy, so she said to Netra and April, "I'm getting ready to go. It's late, and I been up for a long time."

"I think I better be leaving too. Which way are you going, Nestaja?" April asked. "Oh, girl, if you need a ride I can drop you off. Where are you going?"

"I live in the projects."

"Oh, that's no problem, I can drop you off." "Thank you, girl, my car is in the shop."

Once they were in the car, April did just as Nestaja wanted her to do. She started talking, giving Nestaja all the information she needed. She even spoke about how her homeboys had a hit out on a nigga named Jino from Inglewood because she and her sister twisted him, but her homies thought it was all Jino's doing. She didn't know that Jino was Nestaja's baby daddy. She even confided in Nestaja and told her about her kidney disease and that she had to do dialysis 3 times a week.

Once they arrived at her house, Nestaja handed her a piece of paper and told her to call her anytime. She also told her that she was a bartender at the Feline lounge and would like for April and her friends to come and hang out with her one night. That was right up April's alley, and Nestaja kind of knew that when she kept speaking about how she and her friends always hung out at the male strip clubs. April took the number and gave Nestaja hers and told her she was going to call her real soon.

Once April got out, Simone asked, "Who was she, and what was up with her?" "That's one of them bitches that jumped me. I'm playing it cool so I can get my revenge."

"Oh, you sneaky bitch, that's why you wanted the recipe for the juice. Well, I will put a hex on them bitches from my end and you finish them off with the juice."

"Simone, you just dying to do your little voodoo, ain't you?"

"I'm telling you, that shit works. Watch, them bitches are not going to recognize you, and they are going to get real close to you so you can do your thing."

"Well, okay, you do your little voila with your magic wand and we'll see if it gets them close to me. If it works, then I'll let you do something to Reggie," Nestaja said.

"Okay, bet!" Simone said as she shook Nestaja's hand.

Chapter 16

Nestaja sat at her kitchen table, scrolling through her cell phone contact list. Each name she came across, except for family members, she performed a quick mental evaluation. She deleted quite a few because they were dead weight or added no value to her life. Once she was done, she started looking at the most recent and old teenage pictures of her and S Man. She smiled as she turned the pages of the photo album, reflecting on the history they shared and the conversation they shared during yesterday's visit.

"Sis!" her brother busted through the front door yelling.

"I'm in here!" she yelled back.

"What you got going on in here?"

"Nothing much," she replied, closing the photo albums, stacking them together so she could put them back in her bedroom closet. "Whats up with you, bro?"

"I wanna reach out to yo' nigga Craz. I need him to put some money in my pocket. I'm gonna take my baby momma to court and get joint custody of my daughter. I plan on getting out there and getting a job, leaving this hustle game alone."

"I feel you! Me and S Man just agreed on moving to get a fresh start too. It'll be cool for you to come out there and stay with us until you get on your feet."

"Yeah, my nigga S Man don't need to come home and be hanging out in these streets no more. Shit just ain't the same since he left. He might get out thinking it's cool like it used to be and get caught up again."

Ghetto Diva

"That's why I got to get my baby outta L.A.," Nestaja replied.

"My plan for now is to hook up with that nigga Craz and get my bread up so I don't have to stay with you too long when I get out there. Sis, this is going to be the best move I ever made in my life. I can't wait! Arizona, here I come," he stated, full of excitement.

"I'm anxiously waiting too. I'm going out there before my court date to look at some property and see what the job market looking like. I want work part-time for now so I can finish school and have a degree under my belt."

"Sounds like we got a plan. I want to hook up with Craz later on, if you don't mind. I'm always hanging out on the money block, Budlong. I might as well get paid while I'm out there."

Damn! Nestaja thought, remembering she made plans to hook up with Craz

"Me and him supposed to be hooking up around 8:00 p.m., so you can talk to him then." "Okay, I'll be here."

The rest of the day, Nestaja hung out around the house, looking on the internet for jobs and property in Arizona. She called her mom and told her the news and talked to her kids. She went to the grocery store, buying everything she needed to fill up the refrigerator, freezer, and cabinets. She washed the lil bucket and parked it in the garage so Craz wouldn't be asking any questions. She called the day spa to see if she could come in for a European facial, a hot stone massage, a manicure, pedicure, and some waxing. They told her to come in thirty minutes. She took a shower, threw on some comfortable clothes, and headed out to have a much-needed day at the spa.

After a few hours of being there, she was well-relaxed. All of her tension was gone. The only thing on her mind was how she was going to get around having sex with Craz. She really didn't want to go back on her promise to S Man.

When she got home, Craz was already there. She went inside to find him and John in a conversation about making money, so she got herself a bowl of grapes and headed to her room.

About twenty minutes later, Craz came in and laid next to her. He started to caress her body and kiss her neck. She instantly jumped up and ran in the bathroom and began pacing around in circles.

Think, Nestaja, think! Damn, what am I going to do? I can't fuck him. I don't want to cheat on S Man anymore, and besides, my pussy is still sore from the damage S Man did yesterday. Think, girl, think!

"Oh shit!" she screamed.

"What's wrong, baby?" Craz ran to the door asking.

"I just started my period. Can you look in my closet and get me a tampon please?"

Damn! Craz thought as he handed her a tampon.

"Baby, we're going to have to take a raincheck on our evening. You know how I am when I start my period. I'm going to take a shower and call you before I go to bed!" she yelled through the door.

"Okay!" he responded as he walked away, looking like a sad puppy while getting his cell phone out of his pocket to make a call.

"What's up with you?" he asked the person on the other end as he left Nestaja's house. "You going to come over so I can play with that pussy?" he asked. "Good…well, meet me at my house. The key is under the doormat and I'll be there in a few, so be ready to take care of this dick," he said as he disconnected the call. *I'ma beat that pussy up when I get to the house. It ain't as good as Nestaja's, but it'll do*, he thought as he mashed on the gas doing 80 mph up I-110 to get home.

"Damn, Big Daddy Craz, what took you so long?"

"Baby, I was trying to get here as fast as I could, knowing you was going to have this pussy here waiting on me," he replied before he buried his head between her legs.

"Oww, daddy, that's right, suck on that pussy! Ummm, it feels so good! You like the way this pussy taste, daddy?"

"Um-hmm!" he moaned.

"Tell me it taste good" daddy." "Umm, this pussy taste good, Isha!"

"Suck it, daddy! Suck it harder! Ummm, that shit feel good!" "You like how I suck on that pussy, baby?" he asked.

"Yes, daddy, that's why mommy got something special for you," Isha said as she tied a blindfold around his head to cover his eyes. She took his hand and led him to the room. "Now lie down and let me blow your socks off," she said as she aggressively pushed him down on the bed.

She beckoned for her friend to come out of the bathroom. She tied his hands to the bed, and when she was done, her friend began to please him orally. It felt so good to him, his toes began to curl. The feeling was remarkable, but somewhat familiar. She then got up and straddled his dick and began to wind and grind up and down in a circular motion as she tightened up her inside muscles.

"Ooh, shit, baby that feel good," he moaned, ripping away from the scarf she tied him up with. He then took the blindfold off to find Royal, Nestaja's cousin, bouncing on his dick. He made an attempt to stop her, but she remembered her cousin saying he liked it rough and that he also liked to be slapped and talked to, so she leaned forward while bouncing uncontrollably on his dick, saying, "I can keep a secret."

As she slapped him and continued to bounce on his dick, his mind was telling him this wasn't right, but his dick was saying fuck it, you already in her. He laid back and compared Royal to Nestaja in his mind. She got off his dick and lay down while Isha came over and began to eat her pussy. Craz sat back and watched for a while until Isha told him to put his dick in her ass. That was one thing Nestaja wouldn't do. She was a freak, but she would never let him have her ass. So he fucked her from behind while she ate Royal's pussy.

Royal was enjoying Isha's pleasure, but her plan was to get all Craz's attention, so she rose up and began to rub Isha's clit while he continued fucking her in her ass. She then raised up and passionately kissed Craz. She remembered her cousin saying he liked his tongue and neck sucked, so she began to suck his tongue while he fucked Isha in the ass. She worked her way to his neck and began to suck on it until he had a hickey. He was so into the good feeling he didn't realize what Royal was doing.

He pulled his dick out and went to wash it off, and when he returned, Royal and Isha were pleasing each other. They were so into what they were doing, they hadn't realized he was back in the room. They ate each other's pussies and tongue-fucked each other for about fifteen minutes. Then Isha came, so she continued to suck on Royal's pussy until Craz moved her out of the way and inserted himself inside of her. He stroked her pussy real slow and nice the way Nestaja sometimes liked it. After a while, he put her legs on his shoulders and beat it up while Isha rode her face. He pulled out and put his dick in Isha's mouth 'til he nutted.

Royal enjoyed the bittersweet taste of his juices off of Isha's tongue. Then they all got in the shower, washed each other up, got in the bed, and cuddled under Craz.

The next morning, Craz awoke to the smell of turkey bacon, pancakes, and eggs. He got up and there were Isha and Royal in his kitchen, naked, preparing him breakfast and fondling each other. He was definitely turned on by what was before him, so he took Royal and put her on the counter, pulled her to the edge, and pounded on her pussy for about twenty minutes, which caused her to have multiple orgasms, but nothing like Nestaja's explosions. He then got Isha and laid her on the floor and fucked her until he came. They cleaned themselves up, sat down, and ate breakfast.

"So what's up with you, Royal?" he asked "Oh, I'm good!"

"How did you end up in my bed last night?"

"Isha asked me to do her a favor, and she's my girl, so I did it." "But you know Nestaja is my girl."

"Oh well! It is what it is. We're all adults and I know I enjoyed myself. How about you?" "Yeah, I did, but you know that wasn't right, Royal. She's your first cousin."

"You pick a fine time to feel guilty."

"I'm not feeling guilty, but I got mad love for your cousin." "The question is, do she got mad love for you?"

"What do you mean by that?"

"Pay closer attention to her, and you will see for yourself." "Why can't you just tell me?"

"Craz, she is my cousin. I'm not scandalous like that. You have to see for yourself." "Royal, you're not scandalous like that, but I just fucked you and your friend? Tell me

that ain't scandalous."

"Well, I guess we're both scandalous then because we did fuck each other, and we enjoyed it."

"What are you saying, Royal?"

"I'm saying I enjoyed it and we can keep doing it because I'm not going to say anything about either one of you. What she does is her business, and what we do is ours. I'm sure Nestaja don't know about Isha or the five-month-old baby y'all have, do she?"

"No, she don't, and I want to keep it that way." "Well, give me what I want and it will stay that way." "What is it that you want, Royal?"

"I just want your dick. We're already sharing Isha," she said as she leaned over to kiss her. "I want to be a part of the relationship. I want my pussy when I want it and your dick when I want it, and I'm sure Isha don't have a problem with that. Do you, Isha?" she asked as she caressed her breast.

"No, I don't mind!" Isha answered.

"Well, it's whatever with me, but when I'm around Nestaja and the family, I don't want no funny stuff or it's a wrap, Royal."

"Craz, you know you been wanting to fuck me for a long time. Haven't you?"

"You cool, Royal, but I never looked at you like that because of the way I feel for your cousin."

"Well, like I said before, pay close attention to her. Everything that shine ain't always a diamond."

"Well, I'm leaving, Isha. Make sure my house is clean and y'all be out of here in two hours. I have some business to take care of," he informed them while passing them each two hundred dollars. "I'll get with y'all later," he said as he walked out the door.

The girls gave each other a high five and started preparing themselves for some one-on- one action.

Chapter 17

"Hello, may I speak to Taj?" "This is Taj. Who's calling?" "This is Nestaja."

"Oh, hey girl, how are you?"

"I'm good! What's up with you?"

"Not too much, just taking things one day at a time. I have some great information about your case, but I'd rather tell you face to face. When do you want to meet for lunch?"

"What are you doing later?" Nestaja asked.

"I been seeing this guy and we were supposed to go out and shoot some pool later on this evening. Did you have something else in mind?" Taj answered.

"Let's meet for lunch today." "Sounds good to me."

"Meet me at the Red O restaurant at 1:00," Nestaja suggested. "Okay, see you then."

Nestaja hung up her phone, climbed out of her bed, and went to check her mailbox. All her bills she tossed to the side, but the letter from S Man she opened immediately.

"Hey love, I enjoyed our visit on Sunday. I didn't realize how much I missed that pussy. I been thinking about our move, and I know it's going to be one of the best things we can do. We both got Crippin' under our belts and been in it since the 90's, so it's time for change. We know the game of life in our hoods, so now we need to advance to our next stage of life. Together we can achieve a lot. I know things are kind of crazy for the kids, but I know it's just a temporary situation, because I pray for y'all day in and day out, and I know God will never forsake us. Babe, you've done your thing, and I've done mines, but we're still together after all these

years. We definitely have an unbreakable bond, and I will be glad for these last few months to go by so we can put everything into action. I can't wait to play in that pussy all day and night. You think I fucked you good when you came up here, just wait until I fuck you in "our" house. We're going

to be fucking everywhere in every room, all outside in the backyard, in the garage, wherever. It's me and you, baby, from now on. Take care, and stay out of trouble."

Forever yours,
S Man

After reading S Man's letter, Nestaja's pussy was dripping wet as she thought about the encounter they had the other day and all the ones she had to look forward to. She went in her room, took her pajamas off, and laid on her bed. She began to rub on her clit until she was ready to cum, then she went in her bathroom, laid in the tub, spread her legs open, and let the water from the faucet massage her clit. She fondled her hard nipples, thinking about S Man. Then she finger-fucked herself while the water continued to run on her clit until she climaxed.

After self-satisfaction, she washed up, got out, and threw something on so she could go cook herself something to eat. When she came out of her room, her brother John and Asia were in the family room watching a movie.

"Hey Asia, when did you get here?" Nestaja asked.

"I been here about thirty minutes. I was knocking on your door, but you act like you can't hear or something."

"I was taking a bath and I had the radio on. I'm about to make some shrimp scampi pasta.

Do y'all want some?"

"Hell yeah, I do!" John answered.

"I'm cool, I just ate. I'm sleepy so I'm going to lay down on your bed." "Sis, what's up with Akira?" John asked.

"What you mean what's up with her?"

"She looking kind of good these days, and I'm trying to find a female to relocate with me."

"John, you know how I feel about my friends talking to my brothers, and besides, I don't think she's ready to go to AZ. She got a lot going out here."

"Give me her number. I'm going to call her and tell her to come through."

"No, I'm not giving you my homegirl's hook up. Shit like that always go bad, and Akira is my friend. I would hate to off her for trying to play you."

"Man, sis, why you hatin'?"

"I'm not hatin'. I just have your best interest at heart. And besides, you wouldn't hook me up with that ballin'-ass friend of yours, telling me, 'you with S Man, that's my nigga'. Well, you my baby bro, and I said no."

"You on some real bullshit with that one, so I'ma just leave it alone 'til I see her again," he mumbled.

"So bro, when will you be ready to take a trip to Arizona to see what's out there for us?" "Whenever. Just let me know a few days in advance so I don't go out there broke."

"You think you'll be ready to go out there in two weeks?"

"Yeah, two weeks is enough time for me, I'll be ready for sure by then. I can use a mini vacation."

"I'll make us some reservations and we'll just get a rental car when we get out there." "Okay, sis, I'm with that."

"The food is done, but I just want a little bit. I'm meeting my friend for lunch and I don't want to eat too much before I go."

"Yeaaaaah! I love me some shrimp pasta, especially when you put your secret sauce in it," John commented.

"So what's up with you and Craz? Is he gonna put you back in the game?" Nestaja asked. "Yeah, he gon' shoot me a few keys of that good. That'll fill up my pockets since all kind

of niggas be coming through for some weight like that. Only a handful of the homies got weight like that and the ones that do be in traffic most of the time."

Ghetto Diva

"That's cool, just be careful. Akira gave me these pills she got from one of her new tricks. I know I'm not gonna do nothing with them, so dump what you can, and you can keep whatever you make. It's 450 pills in here. It was 500, but I'ma keep 50 because I sometimes run into people that's asking for them. So do your thang, just be careful. I'm going to get dressed so I can meet my friend. I'll be back later."

Chapter 18

"What's up, Jino?" Ghost addressed Reggie.

"What's up, nigga? When you get out?"

"I got out this morning. What's been going on in the hood?"

"Same ole shit. I only been out for a few days myself."

"I came through to holla at you about something," Ghost said. He looked at Reggie's female friend as if what he had to say wasn't for her to hear.

"Hold up one second, let me tell ole girl I'll get with her later." Reggie leaned down in the car window to tell his female friend he'd see her later.

"Damn, Jino, who was baby?"

"One of my lil bitches I be fucking with. But she cool, she ain't from around here, she comes from a good background."

"Damn, nigga, she straight! Do she got a friend, a sister, an auntie? Hell, I'll fuck with her grandmama."

"Nigga, you crazy! Reggie responded. "Nestaja is moving some nigga in her house. I want you to go over there and steal the bucket I just gave her, drive it somewhere, and set fire to it. I also want you to drive by there every chance you get and see if you see that nigga there, and when you do, post up and call me."

"Blood, I can take care of the bucket tonight."

"Okay, well handle your business and hit a nigga when you done, and I'll tell you where to meet me so you can get the rest," Reggie said, handing him $500.

"I'ma go through there about 9:00 and if she there, I'll post up and wait on her ass."

"I'ma call her and make sure she ain't there," Reggie replied.

"Alright, Blood, I'll hit you when I'm done."

Damn, I don't wanna call this bitch, but I gotta act this shit out, Reggie thought while getting his cell phone out of his pocket to call Nestaja.

"Hello?" she answered. "What's up, baby mama?"

"Nothing, on my way to lunch. What's up?"

"I wanna come get you and take you out tonight." "Tonight wouldn't be a good time."

"But I wanna talk to you so we can make a verbal agreement on the kids to avoid all the courts and shit."

"Yeah, whatever, Reggie. What time are you talking?" "How about 8:30?"

"9:30 will be better." "Okay, I'll be there at 9:15."

"Alright!"

***

Nestaja pulled into the Red O restaurant. When she walked inside, she immediately spotted Taj at the bar talking to a very attractive male wearing an expensive designer suit and expensive jewelry.

"Hey, Nestaja, over here!" Taj yelled.

"Hey girl, sorry I'm a little late, but you know how traffic can be over here."

"Girl, I know! I want you to meet my friend. He plays in the NFL. What's your name again, baby?" Taj asked.

"Tony!"

"Yes, Tony, how could I forget? Well, this is my friend that I was waiting for, so we're going to go over here and sit down so we can have our meeting and eat some lunch. I'll be contacting you soon, sweetie," Taj said, walking away with Nestaja.

"Girl, I see you're getting over your divorce just fine," Nestaja commented.

"You just don't know the half of it. I did the opposite. A housewife has been turned into a hoe. I been doing too much, and with my mom being a known lawyer and all, I have to slow down a lot. So I've decided, me and my kids are going to Alabama for a while so I can find myself."

"I see you took my advice on leaving the plastic toys and females alone." "Oh no, I haven't left either alone. I just gained some extras."

"Girl, you are crazy!" Nestaja responded.

"In fact, a friend of mine is working on his baby mother now. He wants me to turn her out."

"Are you serious?"

"Yeah. From what he tells me, she's curious and a freak and he wants me to take her to her next sexual level."

"Taj, you're too much! So what else has been going on with you, aside from your freaky lifestyle?"

"Not much, just been packing for this trip to Alabama." "When are you leaving?"

"Within the next few months."

"So you only have a few more months here in the city?" Nestaja asked. "Yeah, but I'll be back within six months to a year."

"That should be good for you. Ain't nothing like the south."

"Girl, I know! Oh, before I forget, my mom gave me this to give you. She said if you can just get Reggie to sign this paper, he will be giving up all of his parental rights and you will win in court with no questions asked. Once he signs it, go make a few copies and mail one to the enclosed address, make it to Judge Ringgold's attention, and everything from there will be smooth sailing. And as for Josiah, getting full custody of him was a breeze since there was no father's name on his birth certificate."

"Oh, thanks, Taj, I can have him sign this with no problems."

"My mom also had all of your charges dropped, but you're not supposed to know. They'll tell you when you go to court next week. Then all you will have to do after that is go to family court and present this paper with his signature, and you'll be good from there on. Your kids don't even need to be present."

"Thanks Taj, you're the best! Tell your mom I want to take her to dinner or something.

Oh, as a matter of fact, I have a gift card to the day spa. Give this to her. It's for $400."

"She loves this place. She goes all the time. I'm sure she'll appreciate it. But I'm going to have my brother give it to her, because she's not talking to me right now. I thought everything was good until she called me yesterday saying that I've turned into a whore to get over my problems. I haven't talked to her since. Luckily I got your papers from her a few days before."

"Taj, you only get one mom, so appreciate her. She's just worried about her baby, that's all. You should hear some of the things my mom says to me. But I know she means well, so I just take it to the chin," Nestaja commented.

"I know, but for now, I'm having fun, so I'll make sure my brother gives it to her. Here, write your name on the sleeve of the gift card so she'll know who it's from. This is like an all- access pass to my mom. Not only does she love gifts, but she loves when people appreciate the things she does for them."

"Well, I'm definitely appreciative."

"Nestaja, I'm not trying to rush, but I have a date with a friend of mines, so I need to go to the house and change."

"Okay, Taj, it was nice seeing you again."

"Nice seeing you too, and anytime you need me, call me."

"I sure will, and same here," Nestaja said as they embraced each other and went their separate ways.

After having lunch with Taj, Nestaja was feeling good considering the news she received about her case. After running a few errands and making a few phone calls to plan Gina's party, she decided check out Big Bayru's car wash on Central. When she got there, the parking lot was packed with most of LA's finest ghetto superstars. She didn't want to go in the bucket ass car Reggie got her, so she went to Carson and got her car and her partner in crime, Mila.

On the way to the car wash, she updated Mila on everything that was going on except for the fact she had come in contact with the girls that jumped her, and the car wash they were going to was owned by one of their brothers. When they arrived, a female came running over to the car,

"Hey, girl, I lost your number, I been trying to hook up with you. What's up?" "What's up, April? Let me park my car so I can get it detailed."

"Oh, is this you?" April asked, stepping back and admiring Nestaja's luxury SUV. "This is nice. I'll be in the lounge waiting. I want you to meet my other homegirls, Wanda and Tina."

"Okay, I'll be over there in a second," Nestaja replied. "Who was she?" Mila asked in a disgusted way.

"Girl, nobody, just one of these ratchet broads from the block. She be on me because she like a few of the homies and she think she can get to them through me," Nestaja lied.

"Damn, she was on you like you're a celebrity."

"Bitch, I am!" Nestaja joked while they laughed and made their way to the lounge area.

April introduced everyone. "Wanda and Tina, this is Nestaja. Nestaja, these are my homegirls."

Fuck these slob-ass bitches. They just don't know they're in the presence of their soon-to- be killer. I really wanna flat-line these hoes now, but I know I gotta play this shit cool if I want it done right, Nestaja thought as she let off the biggest smile she could muster up.

"Nice to finally meet you. The way April talked about you, and we never saw you, we thought you were an imaginary friend of hers."

"Nah, this is me, in the flesh, and this is my homegirl, Mila. Mila, this is April, Tina, and Wanda."

"What's crackin'?" Mila said as she walked away with an attitude.

"Well, as you know, I'm Wanda, and this is my brother Bayru's car wash. You are more than welcome to anything, and the services are on me. As a matter of fact, I'm going to have the washers get on your car now so it don't take all day."

"Aww, you guys are so sweet! I go back to work tomorrow night. Why don't you guys come up there and have a few drinks on me?"

"Where do you work?" Tina asked "I'm a bartender at the Feline Lounge."

"Oh, bartender? Heyyy, we're there for sure!" they said as they high-fived each other. "Do you mind if I bring my sister? She's cool.

Ghetto Diva

She's usually here, but she had to take

care of something today. Her name is Vickie, and April told her all about you," Wanda said. "Sure, she can come. The more the merrier." Nestaja's blood began to boil. As she stood there looking in the eyes of the girls that jumped her, she knew she had to maintain her composure.

"So, we'll see you tomorrow night," Wanda confirmed.

"Okay, I'll be looking out for y'all," Nestaja said as she walked over to Mila, who was getting a Sprite off the food truck.

"I don't like your new friends. It's something about them bitches that don't click with me. I don't like none of them dusty bitches."

"Girl, trust me, it ain't all what it appears to be. I don't too much care for them either because I think one of them messing with Reggie. After I do my investigation, I'll let you know what's up," Nestaja added.

"I'm telling you, Nestaja, it's something about them bitches I don't like." "Nestaja, your SUV is ready."

"Damn, that was fast," Nestaja responded.

"It better be clean," Mila said as she walked over to do an inspection. "Don't pay her no mind. She's not having a good day."

"I'm not trippin'. We have our good and our bad days. But any friend of yours is a friend of mine," Wanda stated.

"Okay. I know I better see y'all at the club tomorrow night." "Oh, we coming for sure," April walked up saying.

"Well, ladies we've been talking for hours. It's almost 8:00 and I need to get going. So, I'll see y'all tomorrow," Nestaja advised as she made her way to her car.

"It's getting kind of dead up here. Looks like everyone is leaving, so I need to shut down before my brother gets back. But we're gonna to have to hang out. I don't have too many friends, but April speaks highly of you, and from what I can see, she was right, you are a cool person."

"Oh, thank you, Wanda, I like y'all too. We're giving my cousin a coming home party, and I want y'all to come. I'll give you the details later."

"We'll be there," Tina chimed in.

"Nestaja, you're well-liked up here already, and you only been around for about an hour.

I don't know what it is, but I get good vibes from you."

Damn, I love Simone for this. I'ma have to take her on a Caribbean cruise for this one. These bitches really don't know who I am, and they on my bumper like we been best friends for years, Nestaja thought before responding to Wanda's comment. "You know a real one when you see one," Nestaja replied

"I told you she was cool!" April said.

"We'll see you tomorrow," Tina added as they waved, watching Nestaja drive off. "Damn, bitch, what's up with them thirsty hoes?" Mila asked.

"I don't know, that's just how they are," Nestaja replied, not wanting to tell Mila the truth because she would react immediately. She put her car back in Mila's garage, jumped in the fuck it bucket, and headed out to meet Reggie. She decided to pass by the car wash again on her way home. Since the windows had a dark tint on it and it was dark out, she knew no one would see her. As she approached the car wash, she noticed an expensive shiny red coupe and the license plate read "BAYRU".

Oh, so that's Big Bayru, she thought, reaching for her burner. She slowly approached the car and opened fire. She wasn't aiming to hit anyone. She just wanted to cause a little ruckus, so she shot his back tire and the bumper and the rest she shot in the air. Then she sped off, getting on the freeway, making a smooth getaway.

Chapter 19

"Sis, Reggie's outside for you!" her brother John yelled. "Tell him here I come."

"Okay, I'm on my way out too. I'm going on Budlong to make some money. I'll see you later," he responded.

"Okay, bro, be careful," she said as she took a last look in the mirror, grabbed the paper that Taj had given her, and mixed it up with Jasmine's fake private school application before stapling it all together.

"What's up, Reggie!" she greeted him, getting into his car.

"What's up? You looking good as always." *Damn, I hate being nice to this bitch*, he thought.

"Thank you, Reggie, you look good too. And what is that cologne you're wearing? That shit makes a bitch wanna take her panties off and fuck you right here." *Why did I say that? I'm not givin' this nigga no more of my goods. I hate I fucked him when I did. I can't stand his ass,*

Nestaja thought.

"Thank you!" he responded.

"So where are we heading?" she asked.

"I was thinking about going to our low-key spot we use to go to in Marina Del Rey overlooking the water."

"Oh, that's cool. I can use a few margaritas." "A few? When did you start drinking?"

Dummy, I don't drink. It's just a prop to get you where I want you, she thought as she caressed the back of his head, saying, "Well, to tell the truth, Reggie, after our break-up, I started drinking a lot. That's why I had to take some time off from work, to get myself together. But I'm better because now I won't have more than three glasses within a seventy-two-hour period," Nestaja lied.

"So, our break-up affected you like that?"

"Um-hmm, but I don't want to talk about that right now. That's a touchy subject for me," she lied again as she turned the radio up like she was interested in the song that was playing.

Who this bitch think she is turning up my shit to cut me off? I'm going to let it slide this time, and Ghost's ass need to hurry up and call me so I can take her ass back home. I'm not trying to spend a lot of time with this bitch, Reggie thought as he continued to the marina.

When they arrived at their destination, her goal was to make sure Reggie was full of food and liquor. He had seven shots of Jose Cuervo and was feeling good. Nestaja had him just where she wanted him. She pulled out the papers, told him Jasmine had been accepted into one of the finest private schools in Arizona and the application needed to be completed and sent back in a week. Without hesitation, he filled out his portion and signed it, along with the termination of parental rights form. When he was done, she took the forms and placed them in a folder and put it back in her purse.

Reggie was starting to feel Nestaja and was making sexual passes at her. He dropped a cherry down her shirt and started to go after it with his mouth, but was distracted when his cell phone rang.

"Yeah!" he answered.

"Jino, Ghost just got killed! Them niggas from the projects seen him coming down Imperial in your bucket and lit the car up! The nigga had a container of gas in the backseat that blew up!"

"I'm on my way!" Reggie said as he jumped up and headed to the door with Nestaja closely behind him asking what happened.

"My nigga Ghost just got killed by them niggas in the projects. You didn't go over there, did you?" he asked.

"No. What me going over there have to do with Ghost getting killed?"

Reggie had to come up with something quick because he didn't want Nestaja to become suspicious, so he lied and said, "I knew we were going out tonight, so I gave him the spare key to use the car I gave you to take his baby mama to Riverside. I didn't want to say nothing to you because I know you don't like the nigga and you would have gave me problems with letting him use it. I'm just glad you and my kids wasn't driving it, because it happened close to your house on Imperial."

"Nigga, you gave me a car that had heat on it like that?" she questioned in a very aggressive and aggravated tone.

"No, I would never give you a car with heat on it, knowing you have to drive my kids around. What kind of nigga you think I am?"

"I sometimes wonder, Reggie. Just take me home. I'll get another car somehow." "Bitch! My homeboy is dead, and all you can think about is a car."

"Fuck your punk-ass homeboy! I didn't like his ass to begin with, and it wasn't a secret." "Bitch, don't nobody give a fuck about you not liking somebody. Who are you?"

"I'm that bitch. You know, the one you want so bad, but can't have."

"I got a bitch, and she way tighter than you. Nestaja, you just a cleaned-up hood rat - you, your sister, and all them other hoes you kick it with. All you bitches do is chase niggas."

"Reggie, you got me fucked up. I'm far from hood rat material. If I'm a rat now, I guess I was one when you had me."

"You probably were. I just liked your head and pussy. But I didn't like you as a person, and I know you got some sorry-ass nigga living with you. What do that say about you? Is it that bad for you to where you got to pay a nigga to live with you? Why he ain't got his own? Oh, I forgot, you like sorry-ass niggas."

"You sound real stupid saying I got a sorry nigga living with me. I guess that's what I like. Look at the sorry-ass nigga I fucked with for a few years, and you still trying to pursue me."

"Bitch, I don't want you. I'm just trying to be cool with you for the sake of the kids. Fuck you! My new bitch is cool. She comes from a good family, and she don't fuck with a lot of niggas. I know her pussy is all mine."

"Well, good luck, Reggie. You have yet to feel my wrath. And it's all going to come out next week in court. Nigga, you ain't no threat to me or nobody else. Your bark is way louder than your bite. You'll put hands on me, but let me see you run it with one of my homeboys."

"Bitch, go get any one of your homeboys and I guarantee I'll beat his ass! And when I'm done, I'ma fuck you up for putting me through the shit."

"Oh, it's nothing. All I have to do is make a phone call, and its curtains for your bitch ass."

"Nestaja, I'm not about to go there with you right now because I got bigger problems then you and your little bullshit. As a matter of fact, bitch, get the fuck out of my car," he said as he pulled over.

"It's my pleasure!" she replied as she got out, kicking a dent in the side of his car. He sped off, and she called Katrina to come get her.

Chapter 20

Nestaja woke up from a long nap after spending the earlier part of the day getting her nails and hair done and doing a little shopping. It was her first night back to work, so she had to make sure everything was looking top notch. Before she started to get ready, she retrieved her cell phone from the nightstand next to her bed. She had a missed call from Simone, so she called her back anxious to tell her that her little magic trick is working.

"Hello?"

"Simone, I don't know what kind of voila you hit them bitches with, but that shit works."

"I told you! I know they all on yo' bumper and don't have a clue who you are."

"Girl, yeah! They be tellin' me how cool I am, and how they wanna be my friend, and my friends are they friends. I got 'em right where I want 'em."

"So when you want me to start on Reggie?" Simone asked. "Hold on, Houdini, I gotta think about that one."

"Well, I got that plant for you. It works better when you serve it with tea or something hot. It works with other drinks too, but if it's not hot, it gives it a bitter taste and takes a little while longer to work."

"I'll come get it on my way to work tonight," Nestaja replied "Okay, I'll be here. Me and the kids are watching movies all night."

"Girl, you need to get outta the house sometime. Come up to the club and hang out at the bar with me tonight."

"I don't feel like going to the club tonight, but I promise I will be at Gina's party." "Yeah, whatever. I'll call you when I get outside."

"Alright, goodbye!" "Bye, Simone!"

She hung up and packed her bag for work, which consisted of her uniform - a short cheerleading dress - some stilettos, a pair of jeans, and a fitted white see-through T-shirt, some tennis shoes, perfume, and her makeup. She took a shower, freshened up her hair, put on a cute fitted track suit and some sandals to show off her freshly pedicured toes, and headed out the door. She stopped by Simone's and picked up the plant. She put it in her bag and headed to work.

When she arrived, it was 10:00 p.m. and the place was packed. It was her first night back, and Katrina's last night, so it was definitely a celebration in the house. Nestaja went to the dressing room and changed into her cheerleading uniform and stilettos and applied her makeup.

Then she made her way to the bar to find her newfound friends sitting there, patiently waiting for her.

"Hey, Nestaja, you look cute in your little uniform." "Thanks, Tina!" she responded.

"I want you to meet my sister, Vickie. Vickie, this is Nestaja."

"Nice meeting you, Vickie," Nestaja replied, sticking her hand out to shake Vickie's. "You look familiar. Did you go to Jordan?" Vickie asked.

Ooh shit! Nestaja thought. *I hope she doesn't recognize me.* "Yes, I do remember you from Jordan!" Nestaja answered. Although she went to Locke, she wanted her to think she knew her from Jordan.

"You was a cheerleader too?" Vicki asked. "I sure was."

"I thought I knew you from somewhere," she said as she hugged Nestaja like they had been friends forever. "My lil sister and my homegirls speak highly of you. They say you're cool peeps."

"They better speak on me, 'cause I'm always talking about my new friends," Nestaja responded, smiling at them.

"You should come over one day and meet Mama," Vickie suggested. "Sure, I'll come by tomorrow. What y'all want to drink?"

They gave her their orders. She fixed their drinks strong, just like they liked them. They were having a ball with Nestaja, dancing, drinking, laughing, and flirting with the men in the club. Nestaja even gave them a little game and had them getting money from some of the sugar daddies that frequented the club.

Katrina came over to the bar and Nestaja already knew what she wanted. She fixed her cousin a drink and they talked for a little while. Nestaja could tell Katrina was really feeling Deshon, because her conversation wasn't the same and she wasn't at all interested in anyone in the club like usual.

"Nestaja, who's your friend?" April asked. "This is my cousin. Her stage name is Cream." "Hi, Cream!" they all greeted her.

"What's up?" she replied, turning to Nestaja and asking, "Who are these busted bitches?"

Not wanting to tell Katrina who they really were, she lied, "Just some fans that come up here and keep me company sometimes."

"Well, I don't like 'em!" Katrina stated as she grabbed her drink and walked away.

"Excuse me, bartender, can I talk to you for a minute please?" a man yelled as he approached the bar.

"Sure, what can I get for you?" "A pen," he asked.

"Here you go," she said, handing him a pen. "Can I get you anything else?" she asked. "Yeah, a phone call," he answered as he handed her a crisp one hundred dollar bill with his number written on it.

"Well, what is your name?" she asked, admiring his thug demeanor.

"My name is Big Bayru, baby, and I - "

"This is my brother, Nestaja," Vickie said, cutting him off. "I asked him to come up here and hang out with us," she said, grinning from ear to ear.

"I seen you on the cameras at my car wash when I reviewed my tapes yesterday." "Oh, did you? And what was I doing?" she asked, hoping he didn't realize it was her

driving the little the car that fired shots at him.

"Looking sexy, just like you're doing now."

"Thank you!" she responded while stuffing the money in her exposed cleavage.

"Bayru, she's coming over Mama's house tomorrow," Wanda advised him. "I'll make sure I'm there with a gift for my new girlfriend."

"Oh, I feel like family! I get a chance to meet your new girlfriend?" "You already know her. Her name is Nestaja."

"Knock it off, Bayru, I can look at you and tell you got women galore."

"Nah, baby, I outgrew the little boy games. I play in the big league now, and I need a strong backbone like yourself."

"What makes you think I'm strong?"

"Well, for one, you in here on a hustle. You sexy as hell. I can tell you like the finer thangs in life, and you know how to go about gettin' it."

"And you can tell all that from me just standing here in this itty bitty cheerleading uniform and stilettos with my boobs hanging out, in a female strip club working the bar?"

"That too, but I can tell from what I saw on the cameras yesterday. The way you move, the way you dress, the kind of car you drive…"

"How you know I'm not married?" she asked.

"I don't see any stones," he stated as he lifted her hand, looking for a wedding ring. "A ring doesn't mean anything."

"Well, are you married?" he asked. "No, but I have a man."

"Where is he now?" "He'll be home real soon."

"Oh, he locked up. That gives me room to move him out the way." "Well, if that's your plan, you gon' need a 97-ton crane."

"It's like that?" "Pretty much!"

"Okay, I can respect that, but don't think I'm giving up that easy," he advised her as he put another hundred-dollar bill in her tip cut and headed to the stage.

"Nestaja, my brother is really interested in you, and when he wants somethin', he usually gets it. So be prepared," Wanda commented.

"Girl, I'm not worried about your brother. He's used to females falling at his feet. I don't get down like that."

"I feel you. Make him work hard, girl," Tina said as she stumbled over to the bar. "Tina, you had too much to drink," April stated.

"Nah, I'm good. Just give me some coffee and I'll be straight."

"Coffee coming right up," Nestaja responded. She went to her bag and got a leaf off the plant. Since the leaves were crispy, she was able to crumble it up real fine in her hand before adding it to Tina's hot cup of coffee. "Here you go, sweetie, hope this makes you feel all better."

"Thanks, girl," Tina responded.

"It's getting kind of late. I have to get up early in the morning, so we're gonna be heading home," Wanda said.

"Okay. I get off in thirty minutes anyway, but thanks for coming to hang out with me. I'll see y'all tomorrow."

"Here's the address, and beware, 'cause Bayru is gonna be on you," Vickie warned her. "I'm not worried about your brother. If anything, he needs to beware of me. I'll see y'all tomorrow," Nestaja replied.

Chapter 21

"Some girl named Taj on the phone for you, sound like she cryin'!" John advised. "Hello!"

"Hey, Nestaja, it's Taj."

"Hey girl, what's wrong, why are you cryin'?"

"I'm goin' through so much! I lost my apartment. I was staying with my mom, but she put me out and told me she didn't want anything to do with me because I was an embarrassment to her. She had Child Services come get my kids and take them to their dad. I was staying with my brother and his wife, but they put me out when my brother caught me shooting up a few times and having sex with his wife's brother. They're trying to blame me for his drug usage. I'm going to be honest with you. I have a bad drug addiction that I can't shake. I been goin' out with a lot of guys. It's one that I really like, but he don't know about my habit, and I know that he's not gonna wanna deal with me when he finds out. I just don't know what to do."

"You poor thing, you're going through a lot. Well, Taj, the best thing to do is pray, and ask God to guide you in the right direction. Now, I'm not a religious person, but I'm very spiritual. I pray all the time, and it works. It's really hard when you're dealing with your family. As for your male friend, start working on your addictions, and if he's meant for you, he'll go through the rehab process with you. And if he don't, you'll know he's not the one for you. But don't let that get you down, because you're a very pretty girl. If you wouldn't have told me your problems, I would have never known."

"Thanks, Nestaja, I knew I could talk to you without being judged."

"I'll never judge you. We all have our flaws, and I know no one on this earth is perfect.

So you just get yourself together."

"Okay, I will, and again thank you. What are you getting into today?"

"I have to do some running around for my cousin's party tomorrow. You are coming,

right?"

"Yeah, I'll be there. Is it okay if I bring my friend with me?" Taj asked. "Yeah, it's a party, the more the merrier," Nestaja answered.

"Okay, I'll see you tomorrow."

"See you then," Nestaja said, disconnecting the call.

Once she hung up with Taj, she went in her room to get ready before Asia and Katrina came to pick her up. While she was getting dressed, she heard John talking to another male. They were kind of far away, so she couldn't really make out who he was talking to. She went in her bathroom to take a shower, but just as she got ready to get in, someone knocked on the bathroom door.

"Who is it?" she asked

"It's me, Craz!" he answered "It's open," she replied. "What's up, Nestaja?"

"Hey, baby! Where you been? I been calling and leaving messages on your voicemail, but not gettin' a response."

"I been workin long twelve hour split shifts, so all I been doin' is goin' to work and sleep.

I haven't had time for myself. Where you getting ready to go?" he questioned.

"I have to run a few errands and grab me a nice little bikini for Gina's welcome home party tomorrow. Are you comin'?"

"Of course, I'm comin', I took the day off."

"Well, I'm about to get dressed. I have to make a quick run before Asia and Katrina get here."

"You said that like you don't want me to be in here while you're changing clothes or something."

"No, it's not that. I just wanted to prepare you for this," she said as she dropped her robe and got in the shower.

Craz watched as she began to wash her curvaceous body, starting to feel somewhat bad for what he had done with her cousin Royal. Not able to handle his guilt, he told her he was going to talk to John and that he'd be right back.

Even though she was glad he came up with an excuse before she did, she still found it quite odd, but decided against speaking on it. She continued to wash up so she could get dressed and go the projects before her sister and cousin came to pick her up. She got out of the shower and put lotion all over her body. Then she threw on a pair of white skinny jeans with frayed hems that hit every curve from her waist to her ankles, with a cute V-neck blouse exposing her cleavage, a pair of six inch red bottoms, and an extra-large monogram designer handbag. She headed to the kitchen to get a snack, but Craz stopped her in her tracks.

"Where you think you goin' lookin like that? Them jeans fittin' a little too good, don't you think?"

"What are you talking about? You bought these jeans."

"Well, I don't like the way they fit, so you need to go back in the room and take 'em off." "What the hell you on? You never trip on what I wear. Where is all of this coming from, Craz?"

"Shit ain't been right with us, Nestaja. You used to call me all the time, we used to hang out and do things, but now it's all about you. As long as Nestaja is happy, that's all that matters."

"How are we gonna spend time with each other when you are always at work or asleep,

Craz?"

"I don't know, but something ain't right with you. I think you messing around with someone."

"Craz, you need to knock it off."

"I'm telling you, Nestaja, if I find out you fuckin' with someone, I'ma break every bone in your face."

"Oh, so now you wanna put your hands on me 'cause of your insecurities." "Bitch, I'm——"

"Oh, now I'm a bitch?" she said, cutting him off. "Well, check this out, Big Craz. I don't have to stand here and listen to this bullshit you dishin' out. I don't know what you goin' through, but you way out of character, and I don't like it. I'm gonna leave, and when I come back, I expect you to not be here. Goodbye!" she sarcastically advised as she walked out the door, slamming it behind her.

When she got to the projects, Vickie, Wanda, April, and Tina were all sitting on the porch in lawn chairs. She parked her car, got out, and headed over to them.

"Hey, what's up?"

"We're just out here enjoying this nice afternoon weather," April replied.

"You look cute. Where are you going today?" Vickie asked.

"I have a few errands to run. I need to get some last-minute things for the party tomorrow. You guys are still coming, right?"

"Yeah, we'll be there. Is someone gonna be there with some pills, or do I need to stop and get my own?"

"Wanda, you don't need no pills. Yo' nasty ass will end up fuckin' everybody at the party, male and female," Vickie joked.

"I can't help if the pills make me freakier than I already am," Wanda happily replied.

"It do? I never popped one. I was wondering how it makes you feel," Nestaja questioned in an innocent tone.

"Well, honey, let me tell you, it's a mood enhancer. If you already a freaky, horny bitch like me, then it's gonna make you want to have an orgy. I love it. I always experience something new when I'm on one," Wanda advised, but was interrupted as Tina jumped up and ran in the house.

"What's wrong with her?" Nestaja asked.

"That bitch is probably pregnant. She been throwing up all morning," Wanda answered. "I hope she ain't pregnant by Reggie's ass. That nigga is a dead man walking," Vickie added.

"She don't fuck with him no more. That's been over for a few weeks now," April added. "They were kicking it real tough until he went to jail. That wasn't that long ago, so it probably is his baby," Vicki added.

"Fuck Reggie, Jino, whatever y'all wanna call him. Bayru is gonna take care of his ass real soon," Wanda mentioned in a stern tone.

"Nestaja, come inside and meet Mama," Vickie said as she opened the front door for Nestaja to enter.

As she walked in, she was impressed. The house was nothing like she expected. It was quite stylish to be in the projects. Everything was neat and in order - so neat you didn't want to move too much. Nice designer furniture, huge flat screen TV's, nice shiny hardwood floor.

As Nestaja admired the inside, she heard a soft-spoken woman's voice say, "So this is the woman that my girls and now my son have been speaking highly of. Hello, I'm Doris. Nice to finally meet you."

"Hello, Miss Doris, I'm Nestaja," she greeted as she shook her hand. "Have a seat. Would you like something to drink?"

"No thanks, I'm fine."

"There you are!" someone came in the door saying.

"Jermaine, she is not thinking about you," Miss Doris commented, revealing his government name.

"Mama, Nestaja is going to be my wife. We're gonna move to Atlanta and I'm gonna give her whatever she wants. Here, these are for you," he said, handing her a large black and gold box with 42 red roses neatly placed inside.

"Thank you. I see you know how to make a girl smile."

"I'm trying to make your heart smile. Give me a few months, and you're gonna be all mine. I'm gonna take good care of you. Tell her, Mama, I'm a good man."

"Yeah, when you stay out of them streets," she answered.

"See, and a sexy female like Nestaja can keep me out of them for sure," he added. "Vickie, Nestaja is gonna be your sister-in-law," he continued.

"Jermaine, you don't know me. You might not like me next week. I might have a terrible attitude and just be an all-around evil person," Nestaja stated.

"Mama is a good judge of character. Is she cool for me, Ma?"

"I feel she has a good spirit and she comes from a good foundation. She loves her kids and she's a go-getter. She's also very business-minded, but can easily be distracted. She loves hard and long. She doesn't want anyone that doesn't want anything out of life. I think she's a sweet and caring person. I like her."

"I want to love her," he added.

"Wow, are you a psychic or something?" Nestaja asked.

"No, baby, I can just read people within a matter of minutes after meeting them. Was I right?" she questioned

"Can't be any righter," Nestaja smiled while thinking, *This dumb bitch thinks she know me.* "Well, I have to get goin'. I have a lot I need to do today. Here's the address to the pool party tomorrow. I'll see y'all there," Nestaja said as she made her way to the door.

"Nice meeting you too, and you're more than welcome to come by anytime."

"Thank you, Miss Doris, and thank you for the flowers, Bayru - oops, I mean Jermaine." "You might as well start callin' me husband, 'cause I'm gonna be just that, real soon." "Bye, Jermaine!"

"See you later, wifey!"

Chapter 22

"Hello?" Nestaja answered her cell phone.

"Bitch, I keep tellin' you to stop fucking with my husband, but you wanna find out the hard way that I ain't playin'," the raspy-voiced caller yelled through the phone.

"Well, come show me, bitch," Nestaja replied before ending the call. "Who the fuck was that?" Katrina asked.

"I don't know. Some bitch been calling my phone about a nigga, but she won't let herself, or the nigga be known."

"Fuck her!" Asia added.

"I'm hungry. We've been shopping all day. Let's get some takeout from the hot wing place," Katrina suggested.

"That's cool!" they both replied.

"Asia, call the order in," Katrina suggested as she turned around, heading to the food spot. "You go in and get the food, Nestaja. I'll drive up the street to get us something to drink."

Nestaja got out to get their food, knowing she would run into someone because it was a spot that everyone frequented. "I'm here to pick up a call-in order under the name Asia."

"That will be $56.97. Your number is 45, and your order will be coming out soon," the cashier said.

"Nestaja what you doing up here?" a female voice asked.

"Hey, Taj, how you been?" Nestaja questioned, remembering their recent conversation. "A lot better! Came to get me and my friend a bite to eat. We've been out shopping all day.

He laced me with some fly 'fits for the party tomorrow.

"Oh, where is he? I want to meet this mystery man," Nestaja

questioned, looking around. "He's in my car asleep. We been together all day, shopping and getting to know each

other. But you'll meet him tomorrow at the party."

"I've been out shopping all day too. I'm ready to go home, kick back, and read this book I just bought."

"I just got done reading the *Nickerson Barbie* series by Mimi Renee, and they were all good," Taj added

"I'm going to have to get that one. I read a few of her books, like *Pretty Bright* and The Anthology she put out called *Traces of my Lipstick* with four hot female west coast authors. They were all good," Nestaja said.

"Number 45, your order is ready."

"That's my number, girl. Don't have too much fun tonight with your friend. I don't want you to be too tired to come to the party tomorrow,"

"We'll have more fun if you joined us," Taj added. "Don't start, Taj."

"I'm just joking, girl. I'll see you tomorrow.

"Damn, what took so long? We sitting out here hungry and shit, and you taking all night."

"Y'all know they slow."

"Let's stop at the spot and grab some fire before we drop this bitch off on the east side," Katrina suggested.

"Nestaja, when you gon' move off the east side anyway? It ain't like you can't afford it.

Somebody go inside your house and think they're in Beverly Hills somewhere, but when they come out, they realize they're only on 113th and Avalon," Katrina said.

"Yeah, in the belly of the east side," Asia added.

"It's in the making. I'm taking my time so I can get exactly what I want." "Girl, you know Craz will buy you whatever house you want."

"He been acting funny lately. I don't know what's up with him. He been on some strange shit, telling me what I can and can't wear, and how he is gonna break every bone in my face if he find out I'm messing with somebody."

"Nestaja, why you lying on my cousin like that?"

"Katrina, I'm not! He been on some insecure shit, and I ain't with all that." "My brother just loves you, that's all," Asia added.

"Well, when my face is broke the fuck up by your brother and your cousin, you bitches better ride with me when I go bang on his ass."

"You know we got you, but that's not gonna be an easy ride," Katrina stated. "Girl, anything is easy when you plan it right," Asia replied.

"Damn, what's going on over here?" Nestaja questioned when they turned on the block where the spot was located.

"Remember the homeboy Beans?" Asia asked. "No. I would remember a name like Beans."

"Nestaja, you know Beans. You and his sister was real cool. Her name is Yolanda Bates," Katrina reminded her.

"Oh, you talking about her big brother Banadian Bates?"

"Yeah, him. Well, he just got out the pen from doing a hot seven, and they're throwing him a little block party. They invited us, but I forgot to tell y'all," Asia added.

"Banadian was fine and had a bomb-ass body. I bet he is real fine now after doing all that time," Nestaja stated.

"Well, you can see for yourself, 'cause he's walking up to my car now," Katrina said as she got out. "Hey, Beans, look at you all fine and shit. Damn, look at them arms! You was in there working out, I see." Katrina greeted him with a hug.

"Katrina, you doing it like this? I'm diggin' this whip. You looking good too, girl," "Hey, Beans!"

"Oww, what's up, Asia? You thick as a muthafucka, and damn, look at all that ass!" "What's up, Beans?"

"I know that's not Nestaja. Girl, when I left you was skinny with a little booty, but look at you now, all thick and shit with some ass. But I wanna holla at yo' sister Asia. Hook a nigga up, Nestaja."

"Okay, Beans, I'll see what's up."

"Is that Miss Nestaja Simmons, or is it Mrs. Nestaja Gibson?"

Ghetto Diva

"No, it's still Simmons," Nestaja said as she embraced her childhood friend Yolanda. "Look at you! I haven't seen you in years, how are you?"

"Girl, I'm fine, how are you?" Nestaja asked. "I'm good. You and S Man still ain't married?"

"No, but we're still together," Nestaja said as she and Yolanda walked away, briefing each other on what was going on in their lives.

"Yolanda, I know you're glad your brother is finally home."

"Yeah, I am, but quiet as it's kept, you know he was a booty bandit when he was in there."

"How you know?"

"He told me and my mom that he had a male bitch that he used to fuck and let them fuck him, and that's how he contracted the virus."

"What virus?" Nestaja questioned.

"Girl, my brother is HIV-positive, and the doctors say according to his blood count, within the next few months he's expecting it to become full-blown. You know in jail they don't give them the proper medical attention they need."

"Yolanda, I'm sorry to hear that. You could never tell by looking at him. If I didn't know him and I saw him in traffic and he tried to holla, I'd probably get at him. Girl, he is fine, and look at his body!"

"I know. I heard him trying to get at your little sister Asia. Please don't tell her he is HIV-positive. Just keep her away from him. Don't let her fuck with him at all."

"I won't, Yolanda. That's not something you go around telling everybody. I'll come up with something to keep my sister away from him, and again, I'm sorry you and your family are going through that with him. But you don't have to worry about me saying a word."

"I know you won't, Nestaja. That's why I told you."

"We're givin' a pool party tomorrow for my cousin Gina. She finally comin' home. Here is an invitation. Y'all come through. We ain't hung out in a long time."

"I can't make it; I have to go to a wedding tomorrow. But I'm sure Beans will be there." "Okay, call me so we can do some catching up."

"Okay, Nestaja, I'll call you. Here is my number too. Let's keep in touch this time."

"Okay, Yolanda, I'll see you later," Nestaja said as she got back in the car. "Damn, Beans is fine," Katrina said.

"Yeah, he's real fine, but his breath stink and he musty. I wouldn't give him the time of day," Asia said.

Good, now I don't have to figure out a way to keep her away from him, Nestaja thought.

She knew her sister. She would never talk to someone who had bad hygiene.

Chapter 23

"Hi Gina, glad to have you home, I missed you," Niko said, embracing her cousin. "It's good to be home, and I missed you too, cousin. I heard your husband owns a

Mercedes dealership. Cousin, I need a job. I don't want to go back to that place."

"Sure. He needs someone to run the office. I can teach you everything you need to know, and in the meantime, why don't you take some real estate courses? Once you're done, you can come work as a partner with me at my office. That's where the real money is."

"Sounds like a plan. I'll call you on Monday, and we will take it from there,"

"I'll be waiting on your call, cuzzo," Niko replied as she took off her large designer shades and sandals that matched her bikini and headed to the pool.

"When is Tyrone coming with the music? I'm ready to get my party on," Katrina questioned as she approached the bar.

"He said he was running about thirty minutes late, so he should be here soon," their auntie answered as she mixed some more of her special signature tropical drinks.

"What's that you are making, Auntie?" Katrina questioned.

"It's a little something I put together at all of the family functions, which I haven't seen you at lately."

"I know, Auntie, I've been workin' a lot, so I didn't really had time to do anything. But now I'm in a new relationship and he's the breadwinner, so you'll be seeing a lot more of me."

"I know that's right, niece, get'cha money. Don't be like your sorry-ass cousin Royal - don't wanna work, got a sorry-ass man and had babies by him, then he leaves her with nothing, and she can't child-support him, 'cause he ain't never had a job," her aunt added.

"What y'all over here talking about?"

"Hey, Gina. Welcome home. You need to hear this conversation too. You been away for a while so you can use some of this old school game. You see this house?" their aunt asked, holding her hands out admiring her lavish, fully-equipped outdoor kitchen behind her luxury home overlooking the city. "Everybody knows I ain't worked a day in my life. But what I do know how to work is these niggas' pockets. Gina, they gon' be on you because you fresh out. Now, don't you go out there and get caught up with some sorry-ass nigga. Make sure to find you at least a six-figure baby daddy so you can child-support his ass if the shit don't work," she added.

"Auntie, I'm not trying to have kids anytime soon. I want to stack as much money as as I possibly can so I can live lavish like you."

"Well, at least she got her head on right, unlike some of your cousins," another cousin said as she looked over at Royal.

"Please don't start with Royal today. Let Gina enjoy her welcome home party," Katrina added, although she didn't too much care for her cousin Royal either.

"Cousin, you always taking up for that trifling bitch. You know she ain't nothing but a hater."

"That's just Royal. She doesn't mean no harm," Gina added.

"Well, if she rubs me the wrong way, I'ma fuck her ass up, niece or not," their aunt assured them.

"Hey Crystal, where you been, girl?" Katrina questioned.

"At home with Michael. We call ourselves trying to work it out. But I had to come out for Gina's party."

"You never know. It may just work in your favor," Katrina said as she flashed her five- carat ring.

"Damn, bitch, how did you knock that rock?"

"Me and Deshon are getting married. He proposed to me this morning." "Katrina, I'm so happy for you. I finally get to be in a wedding!" Crystal replied.

"I don't want a big wedding. I just want me and him to go somewhere and do it at the spur of the moment. I'll come back and tell y'all when it's official."

"Well, congratulations, bitch, I'm happy for you."

"Auntie, hook me up with one of your specialty drinks. Tyrone finally got here with the music, and I'm ready to parteeee," Gina said holding both her hands up and wiggling her mid- section.

"Here, girl, maybe this will help those dance moves. Somebody need to hurry up and get here and work this bar. I'm not gonna be back here all night. I'm tryna have some fun too."

"Where's Nestaja? She's not going to work the bar?" Gina asked.

"No, she just supplied the drinks. She said she works the bar for a living, not at family functions."

"Um, she's working more than the bar for a living," Royal interrupted. "Royal, please don't start," one family member advised.

"I'm about to slap this bitch," one mumbled to another. "Where is Nestaja anyway?" their aunt asked.

"Probably somewhere chasing Craz after that little argument they had," Royal chimed in. "Royal, how you know they had an argument?" she was questioned by another cousin. "Oh, I just heard."

"You always talkin' about what you heard. Bitch, you need to——" their cousin said as she walked up on Royal, but was interrupted by Tyrone.

"Okay, that's enough, y'all. We're here to party for Gina, not the heavyweight medal," Tyrone said, stepping between the two.

"Fuck this bitch. I'm getting in the pool with Niko before I end up slapping her stupid ass."

"What's wrong with her?" Royal questioned.

"You know she don't like you, Royal. I don't know why you always act like you don't remember," their auntie answered.

"I know she is not still trippin' on what happened back in the day?"

"Royal, she's your first cousin and you had a baby by her high school sweetheart. They broke up because of you."

"He didn't want her ass anyway, Royal replied. "So you decided to give him yours." "Whatever!" Royal said as she walked away.

"Hey, cousin, here is some more ice, cups, and drinks," Nestaja said as she walked up. "Hey, cuzzo, you look cute," Niko complimented as she walked over to get a drink. "Thanks, cousin. I love your bikini," Nestaja replied.

"I don't see how you, Asia, and Katrina walk around in those high-ass heels all day." "It's not really that hard, and besides, these match my dress and bikini."

"Well, all y'all look cute, as always." "You do too, cousin," Nestaja replied.

"We all do," Gina added as she walked up.

"Asia hooked a bitch up with some tight-ass gear."

"Nestaja, Katrina, Akira, Crystal, and Tyrone all put a wad of money in my pocket. Auntie pitched in and got me a condo, and all y'all put together this party for me. Thanks so much."

"Well, I was going to save mines for later, but here," Niko said, handing her a key. "What kind of key is this?" Gina asked, looking at the key fob.

"Girl, you been in jail to long! It's a key fob to a luxury car."

"That sexy black truck sitting out there is yours, cousin," Niko added.

"Oh shit, mine? Thanks, thanks!" Gina screamed as she ran out to see her new ride. Nestaja was heading out front to enjoy Gina's excitement, but was stopped as she walked in that direction.

"Hey, Nestaja what's up with you?" "Hey Beans, I'm glad you made it."

"Damn, this party is off the hook. Tiki torches everywhere, sand, fish, and beach balls, the music is banging… Shit, y'all got a nigga feeling like he in Hawaii somewhere. I should've let y'all give me a coming home party," Beans said.

"Damn, Nestaja, you're not gonna introduce me to your friend?"

"Oh, um, Beans, this is my cousin Lavon. Lavon, this is my homegirl April's boyfriend, Beans," Nestaja said as she walked away with him.

Ghetto Diva

"I knew you wanted me, Nestaja," Beans said, admiring her body.

"Shut up fool, no I don't! I have someone I wanna hook you up with, so don't you talk to nobody else, because I know you gon' like her. Her name is April. She's cute and a freak. So kick back and wait for her to get here. After a few drinks, she's gonna be ready to take you down," Nestaja added.

"Well, when is she comin'?" he wanted to know.

"I'ma go call her now," Nestaja said as she walked inside to call April. "Hello?"

"Hey, girl, when are y'all coming?"

"Oh, we will be there in about an hour. Our plans for today were cancelled, so we're coming earlier than we thought. Why, is something wrong?"

"Yeah, y'all not here. This party is cracking, and I got someone I want you to meet. He's fine, fresh out of jail - which means no drama from a bitch - and he knows how to get his money," Nestaja said.

"If he's as fine as you say, then he might get fucked tonight. As horny as I am, I ain't had no dick in so long."

"Now don't rush into it, because he's boyfriend material and you don't want him to think you're easy."

"Nestaja, where you been? Don't nobody wait no more," April added.

"Well, he is fine with no kids, so yeah, you might wanna grab him while his dick is still tender," Nestaja added.

"Oh, I'm gonna do just that. See you in about an hour," April said as she hung up.

Good, that will keep him away from my loved ones, Nestaja thought as she headed back into the party.

"Hey, Nestaja, you looking good in that bikini, girl." "Hey, Taj, I'm glad you could make it."

"Oh, I wouldn't have missed it for the world. This party look like it's lit! I shoulda left my friend at home."

"Where is he?"

"He's looking for a place to park. He'll be in shortly," Taj replied.

"Okay, I'll be waiting to meet him. I'm gonna be right here at the gate, cuz I see a lot of people are starting to come and I don't wanna miss anyone," Nestaja said.

"Maybe I should go get him. He may have gotten lost or something. I'll be right back," Taj replied.

Nestaja sat on a stool at the gate and greeted everyone with a fresh Hawaiian lei as they entered.

"What's up, Nestaja?" "Hey, girl, how are you?"

"I'm good, trying to make my way to the back where the party's at." "Well, do your thang. I'll see you around."

"What's up homeboy?" she greeted another as he entered.

"What you doin' at the gate? You supposed to be in the back partying."

"I have to stay at the entrance. You know I have to make sure one of your baby mamas don't pop up on you while you back there in your mack daddy mode," she joked.

"Yeah, you stay up here then. I'm going to the back where the action at." "Nestaja, I want you to meet my friend. This is Jino; Jino, this is Nestaja." "Hello, Reggie!" Nestaja said, cutting her off.

"What's up, Nestaja?"

"Do you two know each other?" Taj asked.

"Very well. That's my daughter's father."

"So he's the——"

"One that caused us both to go to jail," Nestaja said, cutting her off again. "And she's the——"

"Bitch that I fucked up and had a baby with," Reggie cut her off once again. "Nestaja, I'm sorry, I didn't know."

"What you apologizing to her for? She ain't nobody."

"I was somebody when you was at my house fucking me in my shower the other day, and I was someone when we went out to eat the night that Ghost got killed."

"Reggie, you told me that you were at a Mexican restaurant with your sister," Taj said.

"Baby, don't believe this bitch. She's a liar."

"Yeah, how do I know you're not lying, Nestaja?" Taj said in his defense.

"Well, frankly, I don't give a fuck what you think, Taj. Both of y'all can get the fuck away from here."

"Nestaja, fuck you and this party," Taj said as she and Reggie walked away hand in hand. "You ain't no threat to me, crackhead-ass bitch! Reggie, if your supplies come up short,

check that drug-addicted-ass bitch," Nestaja said as Akira and her friend Kenneth walked up, asking what was going on.

"What is she doing with Reggie?" Akira asked.

"I just found out she's his new bitch," Nestaja answered. "We need to be beating their asses!" Asia yelled.

"Fuck them! What he don't know is that bitch play with her nose, shoots up, and pops pills like it's candy."

"Bitch, you done got soft," Akira said.

"No, I just handle certain situations different now."

"Yeah, whatever, bitch," Asia said as she and Akira headed back into the party. "Now that's what Nestaja's ass get. What she going to do when Craz finds out aboutthis?" Royal questioned.

"How is he gonna find out, Royal?" their cousin asked. "Girl, Craz knows everything," Royal answered.

"I'm tired of you and your mouth, Royal," their cousin said as she physically attacked her.

"I'm leaving. I don't have time for all of this bullshit," Royal broke away and ran to her car.

"Okay, everybody back inside to the party," one said. "Hey, Nestaja, what's going on?"

"Oh hey, April, nothing worth talking about." *Damn, that was perfect timing! They almost saw Reggie,* Nestaja thought as she greeted them all.

"Where is Tina?"

"She's sick. She's going to the ER tonight," Wanda said. "Bayru said to call him so he can take you out."

"Vickie, your brother is crazy, but I just might do that. April, I have someone I want you to meet."

"Girl, where is he?" April asked in an excited tone. "He's over here. Come on."

"Well, we're going to the bar," Wanda said, heading in the other direction.

"Beans, this is my play-sister April. April, this is Beans."

"Damn, Nestaja, you didn't tell me he was this fine. Shit, look at that body," April said as she gave Beans a hug.

"Damn, lil mama, you look good ya damn self," Beans replied.

"Well, I'm glad you two are feeling each other. I'm gonna mingle and enjoy the party a little bit. I haven't really had a chance to chop it up with Gina."

"Okay. I'll be over here with Beans if you need me," April said.

That worked out good. With her medical issues, drug addiction, and soon to have HIV, this bitch gon' drop dead real soon, Nestaja thought.

"Nestaja, it's getting late, and I need to get home to Deshon and the kids, so I'll see you later," Katrina said.

"Okay. Let's all link up in the morning for breakfast."

"I planned on going to the Harley dealer in the morning. I got my eye on something. " "I'm feeling the bike thang too. I'll meet you at the dealer in the morning," Nestaja replied.

"Okay. I'll see you then, cousin." "Where is Gina?"

"I gave her the key to her new truck and I haven't seen her or the car since," Niko answered.

"She went to get her some dick. She just got out this morning, and party is second on her list, I'm sure," Akira advised.

"Nestaja, me and Beans are outta here too. I already told Wanda and Vickie I'm leaving, and good looking out on the hook up," April said as she and Beans walked out the gate holding hands.

"Well, come on, y'all, let's finish partying. It's only 12:30," Akira said as she and the girls danced their way to the dance area and partied the rest of the night away.

Chapter 24

"What's up, Bayru?"

"Who is this?" he questioned. "This is Nestaja."

"Oh, my wife."

"Your sister said you asked me to call you."

"Yeah, I did. How is your day going?" Bayru asked.

"It's okay. I went and bought a bike this morning," Nestaja answered. "Ain't nothing like a woman on a bike. What kind did you get?" he asked. "A Road Glide," she answered.

"A Harley. Can you ride it?"

"I can ride just about anything," she flirted.

"I bet you can. When you gon' let me take you out?" "When do you wanna take me out?"

"Whenever I can."

"Well, you make the plans and let me know when and where." "Okay, I can do that, wifey."

"I'll be waiting on your call, Bayru."

"It won't be a long wait either," he replied before ending the call.

"Sis, whose Harley is that in the front yard?" John asked. "That's mine. We all went and got one this morning." "Damn, sis, that bike is tight."

"Thanks, bro. Asia, Akira, Crystal, Gina, and Katrina are on the way now so we can go ride."

"I be seeing females in traffic on hogs looking fly all the time."

"We're taking them to the candy shop and let Punchie hook 'em up."

"Sis, I'm so glad you're not one of these chicken heads running around here without a clue."

"I don't have time for that, bro. I got bills and an expensive shopping habit. I don't have time to be playing with little broke-ass boys that don't want anything out of life," Nestaja said as she reached over to answer the house phone. "Hello?"

"What's up, baybeee?"

"Who is this?" she questioned. "It's ya boy, Sweets."

"Hey, Sweets, when you get out?"

"They couldn't keep a real P.I. down, mane. You know the cream always rise to the top, ya dig?"

"So what're you up to?" Nestaja asked.

"Just tryna find me a new bitch. You know all my hoes got cracked when I went down. I need a whole new flock of hoes to fill these stables. Ya dig?"

"I see you still doin' your pimp thang."

"Always, baybeee! Only thang square about me is this room I'm sittin' in. Ya dig? Now peep this here, baybeee, you still grindin' down at that Feline Lounge?"

"Yeah, what's up?"

"What's crackin' with them hoes up there? A pimp need some work. They can be skinny or fat, a dime or a rat, as long as I can make some money off that cat. Ya dig?"

"I see your game is still sharp as an elephant's tusk, but I'll see what I can do for you." "Well, check game, baybeee, a pimp needs that work on deck pronto."

"Sweets, last time I hooked you up with one of the girls in the club, you and four of your homeboys ran a train on her and got her all strung out."

"A pimp had to sample the merchandise before I put it on the market, ya dig?" "Yeah, I hear you. I might have someone for you."

"Okay, bet. I'm at mom's house for now. I'll be here all day networkin'. You know somebody that got a line on them pill joints?"

"Yeah, somebody just came through with fifty for $200. You want 'em?"

"Yeah, grab them for me and I'll shoot you the scrill when you bring 'em to me." "Okay, I got you, Sweets. I'll see you in a little bit."

"Try ta grab one of dem skirts so I can make her famous. Ya dig?" "I'll see what I can do," she responded.

She hung up from Sweets and called her homeboy Chilly Chill. "What's up, Chill?" "Shit, in the studio doing what I do."

"That's what's up. I need to know, how do I put the whammy on these pills?" "How many you got?"

"Fifty," she answered. "Bring me what you got, and I'll swap you for the ones I already got whammed up." "Well, I just need like twenty that's dipped."

"Who you trying to hypnotize?"

"Nobody. I just know someone that outgrew the regular and needs something more potent."

"Well, this is way stronger than the regular," he said. "Okay, I'll be there in thirty minutes."

"Call me when you get in the front."

She hung up and went to her stash and pulled out a clear sandwich baggie with fifty pills in it. She took out twenty and put them in a separate blue sandwich bag and headed to Chilly

Chill's. After she swapped twenty pills with him, she called one of her newfound friends. "Hey Wanda, what's up with you?"

"Girl, bored, tryna to find something to get into."

"Come hang out with me today. I'm just out hittin' corners, tryna see what I can come upon."

"Okay, come get me. I'm at the car wash."

"I'm on the way!"

Nestaja arrived twenty minutes later. When she pulled up, she saw Bayru sitting out front talking to a gentleman in a black van. "Hey wifey, come meet my homeboy, Lil Bayru."

"Hello!" Nestaja said as she approached the two.

"Daaayam, Bayru, you cracked a fine one, my nigga. She right! You got some friends, ma?"

"I'm sure you know my friends already: Vickie, Wanda, April, and Tina."

"Where they find you at? I know you ain't from the projects."

"Okay, man, you doin' too much. You just go to the tow yard and take care of that business with that nigga Jino before he leaves."

"A'ight, Big Bayru, consider him flat-lined," Lil Bayru said as he drove off. "What's up, wifey? You came up here to see me?"

"No, I came to pick up Wanda, but I just thought about something. I need to call my mom right quick. Let me get my phone out the car. I'll be inside in a second."

"Okay, I'll be waiting."

She went to her car and called her cousin Niko. "Hey cousin, do you still have a contract with Reggie to tow cars from the dealer?"

"Yeah, what's up?"

"I need you to call him and tell him you have a tow for him. He needs to leave from where he is right now. I'll explain later."

"We do have two cars that need to be picked up in San Diego."

"Okay, good, tell him he needs to get them and have them to you in six hours. That will make him leave now."

"Okay, cuzzo, I'll call you after I talk to him."

"Thank you, Niko."

Praying nothing happened to Reggie, she took a deep breath, put her burner in her purse, and headed inside, awaiting Niko's call.

"Wifey, come back here with me!" Bayru yelled from the back.

When she walked in, she was surprised when she saw all the pounds of marijuana lined up against the wall. "Sit down!" Bayru said, hitting his hand on the seat next to him.

"Nestaja, I'm really feelin' you, and I wanna let you know who I am. I'm Big Bayru, and I run the projects. I ain't tellin' you this 'cause I want you to be a part of it. I'm tellin' you because I don't want you to be surprised if you catch me in my gangsta mode. Like I said, I run the projects, and no moves are made over there unless I say so."

"Why are you telling me these things?" Nestaja questioned.

"Because I'm feeling you, and I want you to be in my life. I don't want to keep anything from you."

"So you're telling me that you're in a gang? Are people going to be shooting at us?" she asked as if she knew nothing about gangs.

"I don't really have any enemies, but this one nigga that wanna be a shot-caller in Inglewood, we kinda in a funk right now. But I just sent Lil Bayru over there to take care of him."

She slipped her hand in her purse and turned the safety off on her burner, thinking to herself, *I should blow his brains out right now.*

"Baby, you're not gonna answer your phone?" he asked, interrupting her thoughts. "Oh, yeah, I was so into what you were saying, I didn't hear it ringing. Hello?" she answered.

"Okay, cuzzo, he's getting on the freeway as we speak. Is everything okay?" Niko asked. "It is now. I'll call you when I get home, cousin," Nestaja answered before she ended the call and blew a sigh of relief.

"But as I was saying," Bayru continued, "I know you don't know about this street shit, and that's one thing I like about you. I won't have you around any guns or dope. Only reason you see all this is because my boy Smitty is picking it up to take it out of town for me. But to answer your question, no one will be shootin' at us, 'cause I'll never put you in that type of situation. Just give me a chance to show you. I know you got a dude, but I believe all things happen for a reason. It was meant for us to meet."

Yeah, I got him fooled. He think Im a bougie girl living in the ghetto, and I'm going to play this out well. "Okay, I'm going to give you a chance and see what you're all about. But we're going to wait a few months before you get a sample of my bubble gum, and when we go out, I don't want to go nowhere local, because I don't want to run into none of your ghetto girlfriends. I'm not a fighter," she lied.

"Aw, baby, you don't have to worry about that. I got your back, and if you ever out and a female get funky with you, call me and I'll send my sisters. They some project girls, even Tina and April. They not my blood sisters, but I been knowing them all their lives, and I love 'em just like my sisters. But they will fight for you. We don't need you messing up your designer gear," Bayru said as he laughed and hugged her.

"Aw, y'all look so cute together," Wanda said as she walked in. "You ready, sis?" Nestaja asked.

"Yep, let's go!"

"What y'all about to get into?" Bayru asked.

"Oh, nothing, just out hittin' corners," Wanda answered.

"Well, don't hit 'em too hard," he replied, handing Nestaja a wad of money. "What is this for?"

"You may see something you want." "Thanks, baby," she said as she hugged him. "Hey bro, Lil Bayru just called. He said——"

"Sis, come holla at me outside. Nestaja don't need to know about our hood issues," Bayru said, cutting Wanda off. "Baby, if that phone rings, answer it. Just pick it up and say Big B Car Wash. I'm going outside to talk to my sister," Bayru said to Nestaja.

"Okay," she replied.

Nestaja got up to get the remote control and the phone rang. "Big B Car Wash," she answered.

"Hey, Wanda, is Bayru around?" the caller asked. "This isn't Wanda. She's not——"

"Hold on, Wanda, we got a bad connection. I'm going through a tunnel," the caller said, interrupting Nestaja. "Wanda, you still there?" the caller asked.

"Yeah, I'm here. Who would you like to speak to?" "Is your brother around?"

"He's not available right now. Who's calling?"

"This is old man Smitty. Tell dat nigga I'm runnin' a day behind and I'll pick up that package tomorrow night."

"I'll give him the message," she said as she hung up.

She got her cell phone, blocked her number, and called Reggie just to hear him answer the phone so she would know he was really okay.

"I'm ready, Nestaja," Wanda walked in saying. "Okay, let's go."

"Did anyone call, baby?" Bayru asked

"Yeah, some guy named Smitty called. He said he's right on schedule."

"Good! Wanda, make sure you take care of my wife," Bayru

instructed while he watched them walk out.

"I'm glad you came to get me. I was so bored! Do you know where I can get some pills?

I want to pop one and get freaky."

"Yeah, there's this guy I heard of named Sweets that got 'em. We can stop by his spot." "Okay, can you go in and get it for me? A lot of people know my brother, and he don't

know I mess around."

"Okay, I'll get it for you."

They pulled up to Sweets's house, and as planned, Nestaja got out. She laced him on what was going on and told him not to let Wanda know they knew each other. She also told him that Wanda just told her she wanted to pop a pill and get freaky with a few dudes. Of course he said he could make it happen. She told him the pills for his hoes were in the blue sandwich bag, and the regular ones was in the clear sandwich bag.

Sweets walked outside and saw Wanda and he hit her with his pimp spiel. She ate it up, thinking he was really feeling her. They sat there and talked for about forty-five minutes. Wanda was feeling so good that she decided to stay with Sweets. Nestaja left feeling confident about her plan. She made her way to Akira's house, where she found Gina, Asia, and Akira sitting on the porch, catching a cool breeze.

"Hey, I got something up," Nestaja said as she sat down on the step. "What's up, cousin?" Gina questioned.

"I know where about 350 pounds of marijuana is." "Where?" Asia questioned.

"At the car wash on Central," Nestaja answered.

"What the hell were you doing up there?" Akira asked.

"Planning my move. I also been talking to Bayru. That's how I know what's there. I'ma make him take me out tonight, so y'all got to go as soon as I call and tell you the coast is clear."

"350 pounds is a lot. We're gonna need Kenneth to help us on this one," Akira suggested. "The police?" Asia questioned.

"Yeah, I told you he's cool."

"Hell nah, I'm not going!" Asia angrily stated.

"Asia, do you think I would put you in a bad situation? I have done licks with him before, and they go so smooth. We're not going to need any tools at all. Trust me," Akira said.

"Well, you can count me in," Gina added.

"Fuck it, I'll go, but Nestaja, if anything happens to me, you get Kenneth's ass," Asia demanded.

"So I'll have Bayru take me out tonight, and when I call I'll say, 'Mama, I think I found my husband.' Y'all go then. I'll leave a blueprint of the car wash showing you where the cameras are and how to get to everything. It'll be at my house on my bed. I don't want merchandise. I need cash. I ain't goin' with y'all, so I don't expect much. Anything is better than nothing. I'll need it to help me move," Nestaja said.

"Bitch, you really moving?" Asia asked. "Yeah!"

"About time! Where are you moving to?" Akira asked. "Arizona," Nestaja answered.

Asia and Akira looked at each other and burst into laughter. "What?" Nestaja questioned their laughter.

"Bitch, you ain't going to Arizona." "I am. Watch," Nestaja replied.

"Shit, if this lick go well, I'm going with you, cousin," Gina added.

"Y'all crazy moving way out there. It's hot and boring. Y'all will be back in about six months," Asia commented.

"I doubt it. Once I'm gone, I'm not coming back. Me and S Man already talked about it, so it's pretty much a done deal."

"Whatever!" Akira said, giving Asia that she–ain't-going-nowhere look.

"I'm going to hook up with Bayru, and I'll call y'all when it's okay," Nestaja said as she got in her car and drove off.

"Hello?" Bayru answered.

"Hi, husband!" she said in a seductive tone.

"Oh, I see you starting to realize I'm that one," he replied.

"I know it's only been a few hours, but I kind of miss you. I've been thinking about you.

Let's do something tonight." "What you want to do?"

"Let's go somewhere and relax by the beach so we can talk and get to know each other," Nestaja answered.

"I know the perfect spot. Will you be ready in an hour?" he asked.

"Yes, baby!" she answered.

"Meet me at the car wash."

"Where am I going to park my car?"

"I'll lock it in one of the bays."

"Okay, I'll see you in an hour, husband."

The two met up an hour later and went to a nice secluded restaurant overlooking the romantic moonlit Malibu Ocean. They talked, laughed, and had a nice chemistry going.

"You are one of a kind, Bayru." "Baby, call me Jermaine." "Why not Bayru?" she asked.

"That's what the homies call me. You not a street person, so I don't want you callin' me by my street name."

"Aww, Jermaine, you're so sweet," she said as she leaned over and kissed his cheek and then got her cell phone.

"Who are you calling?" he asked.

"Hello, Mama, I think I met my husband."

"Bitch, you late, we at Kenneth's house splitting the profit," Asia said. "Okay, thanks, Mom. I'll be out there in a few days."

"Yeah, whatever! I'm not tryna be on the phone with you right now. This is a lot of shit to put up, gotta go! See you when you come get your cut," Asia said as she hung up.

"Okay, love you too, Ma," Nestaja replied as she disconnected the call with a big Kool Aid smile on her face. "Jermaine, you're really making me feel special."

"That's what I want to do. I want you to always feel like the beautiful queen you are. Anything you need or want, let me know, I got you. The sky is the limit. It don't matter how expensive it is."

"Well, I make pretty good money bartending at the club, plus the side jobs I do from time to time, so I won't be asking for too much."

"You gon' be quittin' that job real soon. You're going to be my wife, so that means what's mine is yours," he said as he leaned over and hugged her.

"I'm a little tired. Are you?" she asked.

"Yeah, I am. Are you ready for me to take you back to your car?"

"No. How about we get a room out this way? I had a long day, and I'm ready to lay it down for the rest of the night."

"There is a nice hotel up the street overlooking the ocean. Is that cool?" "Of course it is. We're just going there to sleep," she responded.

Chapter 25

"I call Nestaja Simmons to the stand," the bailiff announced as Nestaja approached the bench.

"After reviewing case #R102509, the state of California versus Nestaja Simmons, the state of California did not reach a verdict due to the many discrepancies in this case. So by the power vested in me, I dismiss all charges filed against Ms. Nestaja Simmons. You are ordered to report to Family Court at 111 North Hill Street, three months from today. Judge T. Ringgold will be hearing your case at approximately 8:00 a.m. to determine if custody of Josiah and Jasmine will be awarded to Nestaja Simmons or to the other custodial parent. If either defendant does not show up in court, the attending defendant will gain custody of the children. If neither shows up, the children will be awarded to the state of California's Child Services." The judge slammed his gavel, dismissing Nestaja's case.

Although it turned out in her favor, Nestaja was a little nervous, knowing that Taj had something to do with her case being dismissed. She knew she would have to keep her guards up when it came to Taj since she was so weak and Reggie was a manipulator.

***

A few months had passed, and things were coming together as planned. Nestaja, John, and now Gina had gone to Arizona to establish stability before they moved. Nestaja put a down payment on a brand new seven-bedroom, 5800 square foot home. It had a theater inside and a breathtaking resort style backyard with a lagoon-style pool, large lava-rock waterfalls, and a bar. Gina found a job working in real estate with someone that Niko referred her to. Since Arizona was growing and the construction business was booming, one of their aunt's close male friends moved one of his construction companies out there and agreed that he would come down for a few months to teach John and S Man the ins and outs of the construction business so they could run the new location. The girls were doing extremely well after splitting a large profit five ways, thanks to Bayru. They were also enjoying riding their new Harleys and living a ghetto glamorous lifestyle.

Speaking of Bayru, he and Nestaja had been spending a lot of time together. Even though he had taken a big loss, he felt that Nestaja was the one since she didn't run out on him during his major setback. She even gave him back some of his own money by helping him financially, just to pull him closer to her.

One Sunday, Bayru wanted to plan a romantic day for her, so he called her to see if she had any plans. He knew she and the girls would usually be out somewhere on their bikes, but since Asia and Akira were sick with a stomach virus, she was at home doing nothing. She met him at his mom's, and he greeted her with roses and a teddy bear before they headed out to Orange County. They went horseback riding along the shore of the beautiful beach and watched the sunset, then had a nice moonlit dinner at an outdoor restaurant nearby. The evening was going well until Bayru received a phone call. Nestaja could tell by his tone something was wrong. He hung up and dropped his head.

"Jermaine, what's wrong?" Nestaja asked. "That was Vickie. She told me Tina died."

Yes! Simone's lil voila worked after all, she thought. "Oh my God, what happened?" she asked sincerely.

"They said it was natural causes."

"Oh, baby, I'm so sorry. Let's go check on your sisters."

"Nestaja, I didn't want to tell you, but we haven't seen Wanda in about two months. She hooked up with some pimp dude that turned her out. One of my homeboys said he seen her on the track all strung out and shit," Bayru added as he buried his head into her chest, mourning Tina's death.

Good, everything is turning out just the way I planned it. Two down and two to go, Nestaja thought as she held Bayru.

"I'm sure Wanda is okay and she will show up soon," Nestaja said, comforting him. "I worry about her from time to time because Wanda is kinda weak-minded and she's

easily influenced. She needs us for guidance," Bayru responded. "Just pray for her. She'll be okay."

"I can't believe that Tina is gone. My mom raised her from the age of five. Her parents got killed in a crack house in the projects back in the 80's and Tina had no family out here, so my mom took her in. She's been a part of our family ever since."

"I think we need to go see your mom. She's going to need her son right now." "Yeah, you right. Let's get up outta here," he said.

"You can drop me off at my car. I want to pick up something for your mom, so I'll meet you at her house a little later," she said as the two got up and headed out the door.

Once she got back to her car, she called Simone. "Simone, I need to come see you." "Why, what's up?"

"I'll tell you when I get there."

"Well, I'm on your side of town, I'll meet you at your house," Simone said. "Okay, I'm on my way to the house now. I'll be there in about thirty minutes," "See you then," Simone replied.

When Nestaja arrived at her house, she decided to get some rest until Simone got there She was starting to feel sick, so she hooked up one of her grandma's remedies, which was chicken noodle soup with crackers and ginger ale. Her brother John was gone and she was starting to feel hot, so she took off her clothes and walked around in just her panties and bra. She didn't mind Simone seeing her like that since they were best friends, so she knew there wouldn't be any funny stuff.

After about an hour, Simone arrived.

"Bitch, put some clothes on."

"I don't feel too good, and it's hot in here," Nestaja said.

"It's cold as Alaska in here and you're talking about you're hot. Something is wrong with you."

"I probably got a stomach virus from Asia or Akira."

"Well, you stay on that side of the room, 'cause I don't want the shit. But what's up, what did you need to talk to me about anyway?"

"Tina died today."

"You gave her the tea?" Simone questioned

"I sure did. Now are you sure it won't leave a trace?" Nestaja asked.

"I'm more than positive. My people have been using this for years, on animals and people, and no one has ever got caught."

"Okay, Simone, I trust you."

"So has Reggie come and apologized yet?" Simone asked. "No, why you ask that?" Nestaja replied.

"Girl, I put something on his ass that is gonna have him eating out of your palms, but he may try to fight the feeling since I only put a partial one on him."

"Okay, don't go any further than that. I don't want him wanting me and then tryna to kill me 'cause he can't have me," Nestaja said as she grabbed her stomach.

"Are you okay?" Simone asked.

"I'm good. I just feel like I need to throw up," Nestaja replied as she walked Simone to the door. *What's going on with me?* she thought as she ran to the bathroom to throw up.

Afterwards, she laid down for a while to pull herself together so she could meet Bayru at his mom's. She drank some more ginger ale and was fine a few minutes later.

It was a little late, so she went to the 24-hour drug store and got some flowers, a card, and a fruit basket and headed to Bayru's mom's house. When she arrived, she was surprised at the crowd that was there to pay their respects. There were all types of big wheels in front of his mom's house. She got her phone and called her cousin Gina and told her that a friend of hers died and there were a lot of rich men paying their respects. Gina got in her car and met Nestaja there. When the two walked up, all eyes were on them, since everyone else knew each other and they were new faces.

"Oh, my wife is here," she heard Bayru's voice say out of the crowd. "Your wife? Nigga, I didn't know you were married," another male said.

"I'm not, but I will be soon," Bayru replied as he grabbed

Nestaja's hand and led her through the crowd. "This is my wifey, Nestaja, and her friend——"

"My cousin, Gina," Nestaja said, cutting him off. "Oh, I mean her relative, Gina."

"What's up, Gina?" a sexy light-eyed caramel-complected guy said.

"Nothing, what's up with you?" Gina answered while she focused on his gangsta qualities. "What's your name?" she asked.

"They call me Big Cat." "Big Cat?"

"Yeah, that's what my homies call me, but you can call me Brian." "Is your girl here with you, Brian?"

"I just got out the pen from doing a hot ten. I ain't got no girl, ma." "Me too, I just got out from doin' seven."

"Well, we need to get together and make something happen wit' yo' sexy ass," henreplied.

"Let's exchange numbers first and see where it goes," Gina suggested.

"Hey, is that my cousins, Gina and Nestaja?" a loud voice yelled through the crowd. "Oh, hey Royal!" they both responded in a bland tone.

"You know Royal?" Bayru asked Nestaja. "Yeah, she's my cousin. How do you know her?"

"Who don't know Royal's shady ass? I know dat's your cousin, but she messy, and her whole conversation is a lie. You can't believe shit Royal say. She got a baby by one of the homies. That's how we know her."

"I'm not surprised," Gina said.

"Oh, be nice, Gina, that's our cousin. Hey, girl, how you been?" Nestaja said, greeting Royal with a hug.

"I'm cool. I haven't seen y'all since the pool party. Nestaja, looks like you putting on some weight."

"Do it?" Nestaja replied, looking down at her body.

"That's from all that good eating we been doing," Bayru said. "Um, what you mean by we?" Royal questioned.

"Yeah, this is my boo, Royal. You might as well welcome me to the family now, because I'ma wife her real soon," Bayru said, kissing Nestaja on the forehead.

Royal definitely wasn't prepared to hear that. She was heated, and Gina saw it in her eyes when she stomped off with an attitude.

"What's wrong with her?" Brian asked.

"I don't know. I guess she just put her hater jacket on," Gina answered as she and Brian walked away.

"You and your relative kinda look a lot alike. What's her name again?" Bayru asked. "Her name is Gina. Yeah, I know, everyone says that. They always mistake us for each other."

"If she didn't have that short haircut, I would be thinkin' she was you," Bayru said as he and Nestaja walked inside the house. "Ma, someone is here to see you!" Bayru yelled as he opened the door for Nestaja to enter. "I'll be outside if you need me," he said, closing the door behind her.

"Hi, baby, good to see you," Ms. Doris excitedly said as she greeted Nestaja with a hug. "Sorry about Tina. Here, I got these for you," Nestaja said as she handed her the flowers, card, and fruit basket.

"Oh, thank you baby, you're so sweet. My son knows how to pick 'em, don't he?" she said to a lady that was sitting in the kitchen.

"Well, I don't want to keep you. I know you have a lot to do, so I'm going to go outside and say goodbye to everyone before I go in for the night," Nestaja said.

"Yeah, we're just in here trying to figure out how we are we gonna come up with all the money to give her a proper burial. You know what happened to Bayru. Someone took just about everything from that car wash of his. Now everything is just about gone, and this is one time we need it," Ms. Doris said as she began to cry.

Nestaja went into her purse, pulled out two stacks that were folded up with rubber bands, and handed it to Ms. Doris. "Here is a little something. Hopefully this will help you a little," Nestaja said as she embraced Ms. Doris and walked out the door, passing Royal as she was coming in.

"Hey, Ms. Doris," Royal said.

"Hello, baby. Now who are you?" Nestaja heard Ms. Doris ask

Ghetto Diva

Royal.

Why is this bitch always trying to compete? I'm gonna have to play it cool with her, 'cause I don't need her tellin' Bayru nothing about me, Nestaja thought to herself as she sniggered.

"Your relative Royal is something else," Bayru said.

"She's been like that since we were kids. Well, babe, I need to get going. You be careful out here and call me if you need me," Nestaja said

"Am I gonna see you tomorrow?" "Sure you are, babe."

"Okay, drive careful."

"I will. Where did Gina go?" Nestaja asked.

"Here I am, cousin," Gina said, getting out of an expensive black wagon. "I was sitting in Brian's wagon talking. Are you ready to go?"

"Yeah, I don't feel too good. I think I got that stomach virus. You cool?" "Yeah, I'm cool, but we came together, so we gotta leave together." "No, you stay and get to know Brian. He's cute, Gina."

"I know, that's why I'm leaving. If he wants me, he needs to chase me a little." "Look at you, tryna have a little game." Nestaja smiled.

"I wonder who she got that from?" Bayru asked.

"I don't know. It didn't come from me," Nestaja answered with a sly smile on her face. "Baby, you go home and get some rest so you can feel better."

"Okay, see you later, babe. Gina, I need to talk to you before I go. Bayru, I'll call you when I get home to let you know I made it safely," she said as she got in her car, unlocking the other door so Gina could get in.

"What's up, cousin?"

"I need to make sure Royal's ass don't tell Bayru nothing about me. He's cool, but I'm only dealing with him for revenge. I'm after his sisters. He thinks I'm homie and that I don't have any street savvy since I talk proper when I'm around him. So, cousin, I'ma need your help with this one. Royal's baby daddy got killed and his people moved to Chicago, so there is no reason she needs to be over here."

"Okay, cousin, I'll come up with something. I'll come through here from time to time. Brian said she's over here just about every day, so I'll feel her out and see where her head is. You go home and get some rest. I'm about to head to the house myself. I got a few things I need to do early in the morning."

"Okay, Gina, I'll see you later."

Chapter 26

A few days had passed, and things were pretty much the same. Nestaja was waiting on her court date to come around. She and the girls were enjoying their bikes and hanging out with some of the bike clubs. All except Crystal. Her boyfriend Michael was offered a supervisor position in Seattle that was paying close to 100k a year, so they decided to move and continue to work on their family. Bayru was enjoying getting to know Nestaja by spending a lot of time with

her. When he wasn't with her, he was hustling, trying to get his pockets back right.

Wanda came to Tina's funeral looking horrible, and she disappeared later that night.

April and Beans had gotten an apartment together and were enjoying each other sexually, mentally, and emotionally. Vickie was hustling with her brother, helping him get back in the game. Reggie found out about Taj's drug addiction and stopped dealing with her. Craz, Isha, and Royal were enjoying their newfound relationship, which Nestaja still didn't know about. Nestaja decided to stay at home for a few days, since she had not been feeling well. She woke up one morning and headed straight to the bathroom.

Point the absorbent tip directly in the urine stream for at least 7-10 seconds to allow the sample into the testing device, Nestaja read as she squatted over the toilet, aiming her early- morning pee towards the absorbent tip.

Negative: Not pregnant, only one color band will appear. Positive: Pregnant, two color bands will appear.

Please allow 5-10 minutes to complete the test reaction.

It's only been a few seconds. After I wash my face and brush my teeth, the results should be clear, Nestaja thought as she washed her hands and did a few other things to kill time, since she was anxious to get the results. After she was done, she took a peek and there were two lines.

"Oh my God!" she said out loud. *This can't be right*, she thought.

What am I going to do? Who's the daddy? I had sex with S Man a few days after Reggie, and I'll be damned if I have another baby by Reggie's triflin' ass. I can't do this to S Man. I love him, and promised him I would do as he expected. What am I going to do? she thought as she laid across her bed in deep thought until someone knocked on her bedroom door.

"Come in!" she yelled.

"Sis, I just wanted to let you know me and Akira are gonna hang out for a few hours, then I'll be going on the block. I'll be back later," John said.

"Okay, bro, y'all have fun. I'm not feeling well, so I'll be right here lying down. See you later."

"Okay, sis, I'll be in later on tonight," John said as he walked out the door.

A few hours had passed, and Nestaja decided to get up and make her grandma's famous get-well-quick remedy again. As she pulled herself up and stumbled to the kitchen, her house phone rang.

"Hello?" she answered. "Hi, Mama!" Josiah said. "Hey, son, how are you?"

"Fine. We going to Atlanta with Grandma tomorrow." "Atlanta? What's out there?"

"She gotta preach at her friend's church."

"Oh, that's good. How you and Jasmine been doing? Mommy misses you guys."

"We're fine! We miss you too."

"Is Jasmine still peeing on herself?" Nestaja asked.

"No. We like it out here. Mama, are we going to get that big house we looked at when you were out here?" Josiah asked.

"Yeah, I already gave them the deposit."

"Uncle John and Cousin Gina going to stay with us?"

"Yeah, but only for a few months until they get their own place." "When are you coming back out here?" Josiah asked.

"After I go to court for this custody hearing. Where is Jasmine?"

"She's asleep. We went swimming earlier, and she got tired. Grandma wants to talk to you, Mama," Josiah said.

"Okay, let me talk to her." "Hello?"

"Hi, Mama!"

"What's going on with you, Nestaja?" her mom asked.

"Oh, not much, just getting things in order to come out there." "Where is John?" she asked.

"He and Akira went on a little lunch date. He'll be back later on tonight."

"I don't know what it is, but I feel something ain't right. I called all my kids yesterday and today, cuz something don't sit right with me in my spirit. God is not pleased with the activity that some of y'all are into."

"Well, Mama, everything is fine here. Things are going according to the plan. Once the house is done, me, S Man, Gina, and John will be out there."

"Have you been going to church?" "Not really, I——"

"I know you're not saying you don't have time, Nestaja."

"No, I always have time for God. I just haven't been to church."

"Nestaja, you been going to that church for years. Don't stop now. I'm sure God has a message for you."

"I know, Mom, and Bishop Jones is a very powerful speaker. I get a message every time I go. I don't have an excuse. I just been lazy. I'ma go Sunday."

"Yeah, you go, and take Asia, John, Gina, and whoever else you can with you." "I will. Akira goes all the time," Nestaja replied.

"Well, that's good, you need to go with her."

"Okay, Mom, I'll go. I'm not feeling too good right now, so I'm going to hang up and get some rest," Nestaja said.

"You're not pregnant, are you?" her mom asked.

"Mama, I——" *Beep!* "Oh, Mama, I got to go, that's my other line ringing." "Okay, now you heard what I said. YOU BE IN CHURCH ON SUNDAY!"

"Okay, love you, Mama, gotta go!" Nestaja said as she hung up to answer the other line.

She lied to get her mother off the phone.

While Nestaja was at home trying to fight her pregnancy sickness, someone knocked at her door. "Who is it?" she yelled.

"Jino!" he answered.

Aww, what does he want? I'm not in the mood for him and his bullshit today, she thought as she opened the door.

"What's up, baby mama?" "What's up, Reggie?"

"I can't come in?"

"Reggie, what do you want?"

"I just want to talk to you, that's all." "About what?" she asked as she let him in.

"Nestaja, ain't no reason for us to be at each other's throats the way we have been. We got two kids together and a business that we need to decide what we're gonna do with, and life is too short to be beefin' with loved ones. I'm out here in these streets every day, and it ain't guaranteed that I'll make it back home. So for the sake of the kids, let's call a truce," he said as he stuck his hand out to shake hers.

"Reggie, what are you up to?" she asked.

"Honestly, I don't even know. I wanna go upside your head for all the bullshit we've been through these past years, but the man in me won't let me fuck you up. I don't want us to have beef with each other no more, so let's squash it. We go to court in a few weeks, and we can resolve this issue without having the system all in our business. We both made some life-altering mistakes that we can't take back, so the only thing left for us to do is get along."

"Reggie, I'm cool with that."

"So no more bullshit from here on out?" Reggie stated.

"No more, and hopefully, we get along better this way. So what are we going to do with our business, Bump and Jump?" Nestaja asked.

"Do you want to sell it?" Reggie asked.

"Yeah, I think that will be the best thing to do. I'll run an ad in the paper this weekend for the jumpers, helium tanks, popcorn, cotton candy, and hot dog machines, and we split the profit 50/50. The tables and chairs, I think we should donate them to a school or church."

"Okay, run the ad with my cell phone number and I'll let you know when we sell 'em," Reggie replied.

"Sounds like a plan," Nestaja replied.

"So what's up with you and Craz?" Reggie asked. "Nothing. What's up with you and Taj?"

"Nothing. That bitch better be glad I didn't kill her for stealin' my shit. I didn't know the bitch was strung out like that."

"Sorry you had to find out the hard way," Nestaja replied. "How you know her?" Reggie asked.

"I met her when we went to jail," Nestaja answered. "You know she on pussy. Y'all ain't never kicked it?"

"No! She was just someone I met and she seemed cool, so we exchanged numbers." "Well, that ain't what she told me," Reggie said.

"What do you mean by that?"

"She told me she tried to get at you, but you shot her down." "I did, Reggie. I'm not into females like that."

"Nestaja, you a freak. You mean to tell me you ain't never thought about being with a female?"

"Yeah, I thought about it, and that's how I know I don't want to."

"So if I was to bring a bad bitch to you and she wanted to eat your pussy, you wouldn't let her?"

"Reggie, why are you even gettin' at me like this? I need to lay down. I don't feel too good."

"Yeah, you go get some rest and think about what I said. I may have someone for you." "I'm not thinking about nothing. We're not goin' there, Reggie, because when we start

fucking, we always fight later." "We didn't last time."

"Not immediately after, but we did get into it," she said as he opened the door for him to exit.

"You're putting me out?"

"No, I told you, I don't feel good," Nestaja said as she made an attempt to run to the bathroom. But she didn't quite make it, and she threw up on Reggie's shoe and all over her floor.

"Are you pregnant?" Reggie asked.

"Reggie, just go. I need to lay down," Nestaja said as she lightly pushed him out the door and tossed him a towel for his shoe.

Chapter 27

essage #1: "Nestaja, this is my fourth time calling. Someone wanna get the party supplies. You need to get at me ASAP so we can go get the stuff outta storage. Call me back!"

Message #2: "Nestaja, this is Akira. John asked me to call you and let you know we'll be back sometime tonight. We're in Santa Barbara."

Message #3: "What's up, Nestaja? Long time no hear from you. Just in case you don't catch my voice, this is Craz. I'm just checkin' on you, since you don't know how to call a nigga."

Message #4: "Nestaja, this is Vickie. Just callin' to see what's up wit'cha and see if we still going to the function in Compton?"

"Damn, I forgot that's today," Nestaja thought out loud.

Message #5: "Nestaja, this is your boss. You haven't been to work in a few weeks. What's up with you, girl? Call me."

After Nestaja checked her messages, she forced herself out of bed. She washed up and made an attempt to go to the kitchen to make some breakfast, but ended up back in the bed. She laid there praying S Man was the father. She felt this was a punishment from God for her promiscuous behavior, so she feared getting an abortion. While deep in thought, her phone rang. "Hello?" she answered.

"Waddup, biootch?" Asia yelled into the phone. "Nothing, laying down."

"Damn, you still sick?"

"Yeah, and I'm probably gonna be for the next 7-8 months," Nestaja answered. "Owww! S Man gon' kick yo' ass."

"Why would he do that? He don't wanna hurt his unborn child," Nestaja stated.

"How you get pregnant by him? Y'all ain't married, so you can't get a conjugal visit." "But we can get a sneaky freaky one," Nestaja replied.

"So what are you gonna do?"

"I'm gonna take my prenatal pills and continue to be a good mother to my children." "Have you told him yet?"

"I haven't heard from him. I wrote him, so he should be calling soon."

"Before you think about havin' another one, you need to get back the ones you already have," Asia sarcastically added.

"What do you mean get 'em back? I never lost 'em, I know exactly where they are," Nestaja shot back.

"What you need to do is get in touch with Josiah's real father. Reggie ain't his daddy.

You gon' have the boy all confused."

"I'm not getting in touch with nobody. If he wanna see or talk to Josiah, he knows exactly how to find him. He got Daddy and Mama's number, and he knows where I live, so he has no excuse. Josiah knows who his daddy is."

"You stupid! My poor nephew is all confused."

"Asia, I don't know why I'm wasting my time talking to you anyway. You see everything one-sided," Nestaja added before she slammed the phone in Asia's ear.

Pregnant bitch! It ain't my fault her nose is about to spread as wide as her ass, Asia thought as she placed the phone back on the charger. Asia had no children, so she could only imagine what her sister was going through. She did, however, recall her grandmother telling her cousin Donna about drinking red raspberry tea during her pregnancy. It was high in iron, calcium, and helped with nausea. It could also make the labor easier, since it also toned the uterine muscles. She decided to go get some of the red raspberry tea and take it to her sister. When Asia got to the health food store, she ran into Craz.

"Hey, sis!" he said, greeting her with a hug, but seeming a bit apprehensive.

"What's up, brother?" she responded, noticing how he was looking around as if he didn't want to be seen. She didn't have time to investigate, so she paid for the tea and headed out of the store. On her way out the door, she ran into her cousin Royal.

"What's up, Royal?" Asia greeted her. "Hey, what's up Asia?"

"Nothing much, up here to get some tea for Nestaja's pregnant ass."

"Aww, my cousin is about to have another baby? I know her and Craz are happy about their new little blessing," Royal probed, waiting on a response.

"No, her and S Man are finally havin' a baby together. They been together so long, even I'm happy about it."

"What happened with her and Craz? I thought they were tight," Royal continued, probing.

"Cousin, you know Nestaja. I'm sure he is somewhere in the cut. But let me get this to her before she throws up all her insides," Asia said as she got in her car, not knowing that she had just given Royal all the information she needed to make her day.

***

"Sis, I got something for you," Asia said while constantly ringing on the doorbell. "Damn, Asia, why you ringing the doorbell like you're running from the police?" Nestaja

asked as she let Asia in.

"Here, bitch, I got this for you. I remember Grandma giving this to Donna when she was pregnant with BJ, and it worked for all that sick shit you're going through," Asia said as she handed Nestaja a bag filled with red raspberry tea.

"Aww, thank you, bitch, you do have a heart," Nestaja said as she reached over to hug her sister. "I'ma drink this tea now so I can get out of this house. I been down for too many days."

"What you think S Man gon' say?" Asia asked.

"I'm sure he gon' be happy, because we always wanted kids together, but seems like when we had those short separations, I had babies by someone else and so did he. But through it all, we still hung in there, and no matter what. I'm his baby momma and he my baby daddy."

"What you gon' tell Craz?"

"I ain't been fuckin' with him. Me and Craz ain't never during all the time I been dealing with him had an argument, and now all of a sudden he wanna come over and trip on the clothes I wear, and he the one bought them."

"I just saw him at the health food store. He was acting a bit strange."

"He cool and all, but I think it's time I let go."

"What if he takes your car back?"

"I don't think he'll do that, and besides, it's in my name, so he can't take it back." "I don't care what y'all go through. He still gonna be my brother."

"That's cool. He's a good person. Just best to be friends instead of in a relationship.

Umm, this tea tastes pretty good. I hope it kicks in quick so I can get my hair done then swing by the nail shop before I go to this function tonight," Nestaja said, sipping the tea.

"You talking about the one in Compton? Naw, I'm good. I'm gonna hit up the bike set. Crystal's out here for a few days. Michael gave her a 48 hour pass so we gon' turn all the way up."

"Y'all have fun. I'll be back on the scene after I have my baby." "Well, I'm outta here. I got some errands to run. I'll call you later."

"A'ight, thanks for the tea, sis. I needed this. I'm starting to feel better already," Nestaja added as she closed the door.

She got her phone and called Vickie to let her know she was still going to the function. She also called her job and informed them she was pregnant and that she was taking a leave. Then she returned Craz's call, but she didn't get an answer, so she left him a message letting him know she did return his call. She also called her stylist to make an appointment to get her hair done. Since the appointment was for later in the day, she decided to go to the nail shop while it was still early. She got dressed and headed out to take care of her beauty necessities.

Chapter 28

Nestaja decided to drive her new car, since she had gotten it detailed at the car wash across the street from the hair shop while she got her hair done. It was still hot out. She got dressed in some distressed stretch-denim shorts with a colorful designer shirt that fit loosely in the mid-section, but tight up top, with a lace up front that complemented her cleavage and a pair of designer jeweled toe-ring sandals. She grabbed her handbag and headed out the door.

"Vickie, Nestaja is here to pick you up!" Ms. Doris yelled up the stairs as she welcomed Nestaja inside. "How's my future daughter-in-law doing?"

"I'm fine, Ms. Doris, just trying to get out and have a little fun." "You look cute tonight, as always."

"Thank you, Ms. Doris."

"Baby, call me Mama. You family." "Okay!" Nestaja nonchalantly responded.

"I heard you weren't feeling well. That flu has been going around, but I'm glad you're better," Miss Doris said while looking up the stairs.

"I don't know what's taking Vickie so long. Let me go see what the problem is."

After Ms. Doris went upstairs, Nestaja heard someone outside fumbling with some keys and the door like they were having a hard time getting in. After a few seconds, the door swung opened and Wanda appeared. "Hey, Nestaja, I didn't expect to see you here."

"Damn, Wanda, look at you! How you get so damn skinny? What are you doing?" Nestaja asked while picking grass and weeds out of Wanda's hair.

"Oh, umm, I been stressed out."

"Wanda, I know I haven't been around that long, but I feel like you're my sister. You can tell me, because your weight loss don't look healthy."

"Sis, I'm addicted to more drugs than I can handle. I'm working for Sweets now, so I'm making a little money. I just can't shake the drugs. I been stealing so I can get high. I don't know what to do."

"Wanda, you know what to do. The question is, are you ready to do it?" "Honestly, no. I love the life I'm living right now."

"Are you serious? Your mother is going to be hurt." "Is she here?" Wanda asked.

"Yes, she's upstairs. Well, I'm going to leave before she comes down. Don't tell her I was here, and please don't tell my brother," Wanda begged.

"I won't, but you need to get it together. You look a mess," Nestaja responded as she watched Wanda rush into the kitchen, grabbing a bag and stuffing it with a little bit of everything she could in thirty seconds. Then she crept out the front door.

When Ms. Doris came downstairs, she noticed the look on Nestaja's face, so she immediately asked what was wrong.

"Just being in this house reminds me of Tina. I miss her so much, that's all," she lied. "Oh, baby, bless your heart. It's okay. We all miss Tina. Now I know you don't want

Jermaine to see you looking all sad, so go in the bathroom and pull yourself together, because he's around the corner and should be walking in soon."

I love Simone for this voila. It really works. Hmm, Ms. Doris is supposed to be a good judge of character, but she sho' ain't picked up on me getting revenge on these hoes and her son. And poor April, she's gonna die a slow death after Beans infects her with the virus along with her other ailments, Nestaja thought.

"Thank you, Ms. Doris," Nestaja replied as she went into the bathroom to freshen up. When she came out, Vickie sat in the living room talking to her two friends, and to

Nestaja's surprise, they were dressed pretty decent.

"Nestaja, I want you to meet my homegirls. This is Roslind and Danielle."

Ghetto Diva

Nestaja greeted them both while admiring their ensembles. Roslind wore an expensive couture summer dress that hit every curve on her body with a pair of red bottom sandals and an oversized designer handbag. Her long, flowing jet-black weave complimented her chocolate skin tone. Danielle wore a pair of designer distressed jeans with a matching ruffled halter top that showed off her firm, braless 38DD's, with a pair of designer sandals and a matching handbag.

When Nestaja looked at Danielle's body, she thought of the girl Deelishis from the *Flavor of Love* show. Even Vickie was looking fly. She wore a black, fitted romper with a wide white belt with 2 large G's on it and a pair of white studded strappy sandals and a white handbag that matched the belt.

"We look too fly to be standing in the living room. Let's get out and get it in," Nestaja commented.

"Bayru just called. He had to go back to the car wash to meet someone. He said to come up there before we head out," Vickie informed.

"Can we stop at the store first? I gotta get my drink so I can feel good when we get there," Roslind added.

"No problem," Nestaja responded.

When they got to the store, there was a big expensive luxury car with New York plates parked out front. As they approached the door, two fine dark-skinned men were coming out.

"Hey, sexy gal!" one said with a strong Jamaican accent.

"Where you ladies headed?" the other one asked, sounding like a New Yorker. "I wish we were going with y'all," Danielle seductively responded.

"We not from out here, but our boy is giving a grown and sexy party tonight in Inglewood. There's gonna be plenty of food and drinks. Only thing else we need is you ladies to bless the party with y'all's presences," New Yorker stated.

"Nestaja, let's go there instead," Roslind suggested.

"Yes, ma, I really wanna see you there," New Yorker added while licking his lips, looking back and forth from Nestaja to Danielle.

"We can do that. It's always functions in Compton. We'll catch the next one," Nestaja replied.

"Here's the address," Jamaican said, handing Vicki a piece of paper with the address on it. "First, we gotta stop at your hubby's car wash, then we can head out to Inglewood," Vickie hated.

"Oh, I'm sorry, I didn't know you were married. Tell your husband he can come too. It's gonna be a cool party, and I really wanna see you there," New York said, looking at Danielle's nipples through her shirt.

They accepted the invite, then headed to pay Bayru a visit before making their appearance in Inglewood.

"What up, sexy?" Lil Bayru spoke, gazing into Roslind's eyes.

"Lil Bayru, you know I'm too much woman for you," Roslind responded. "I'm a grown-ass man, baby, I can handle it."

"Is that right?"

"I can show you better than I can tell you," he flirted. "You talk a good one," she replied.

"I can back it all up, too. You gon' be my baby momma real soon gettin' at me like that," he said to Roslind as Big Bayru walked up behind him.

"Where y'all goin'?" he asked.

"These niggas from out of town invited us to a party in Inglewood. They look like some ballin'-ass niggas too. You and a few of the homies should come through. You might be able to get an outta town plug," Vickie advised.

Here this hatin'-ass bitch goes running her mouth again. How her dumb ass gon' invite some niggas to anotha nigga's party?

"This in Inglewood family hood," Lil Bayru said, looking at the address Vickie gave him.

"Just 'cause it's in family hood don't mean it's a family party," Danielle added.

"I don't care what kinda party it is. As long as my wifey there, I'm there. Give me about an hour to shut the car wash down and I'll meet y'all there," Bayru said.

When they got to the party, all eyes were on them. There was a cool vibe: music playing, people dancing, and the smell of medical marijuana filled the air. You could tell by the extravagant jewels, expensive whips parked outside, and the large bets being placed on the pool table that ballers were in the house.

New York walked up and grabbed Danielle's hand, leading her to the dance floor while the other girls mingled. About forty-five minutes later, Bayru walked up to Nestaja, who was dancing with a tall, light-skinned, ballplayer-looking dude. She wasn't feeling him, so she was happy to see Bayru. As soon as she was ready to sit down, one of YG's songs came on and she had to get it in one last time.

"Hey Blood, ain't that that bitch Nestaja?" one of Jino's homies named Nutty Boy asked.

"Yeah, that's that bitch, and she dancing with that nigga Bayru," Klayron answered. "That nigga Bayru put the hit out on Jino and had something to do with Ghost getting

killed," Nutty Boy advised.

Klayron grabbed his .44 Magnum from his waist, heading to the dance floor, opening fire. Lil Bayru, who was dancing with Roslind, pulled out his .357 automatic and started blazing. Big Bayru shoved Nestaja out of the line of fire and pulled his Desert Eagle from his back. Bullets riddled what was once the dance floor, hitting the innocent while aiming at their intended targets. Through all the commotion, Nestaja saw the perfect opportunity. She pulled out her .380 and busted on Vickie aiming at her mid-section while managing to get out of the crossfire and to her car without being noticed. *I hope I got Vickie and somebody got Bayru, because I'm tired of this lifestyle. S Man is coming home soon I don't want him gettin' caught up over my bullshit. I'ma kick back for a few days and focus on me and my family,* Nestaja thought as the sounds of her cell phone ringing interrupted her thoughts.

"Hello?"

"You still in Compton?" Asia asked

"No, I ended up doin something else, but I'm headed to the house now. Why, what's up?"

"We are hanging out at downtown L.A. on the rooftop having some drinks. Come up here."

"Which one y'all at?"

"At the JW. C'mon."

"Who's we? I thought y'all was goin' on the bike set."

"The police turned it out early. It's Me, Crystal, Katrina, Gina, and Akira."

"Crystal and Katrina hanging out? I gotta see it to believe it. I'm on my way."

It had been awhile since they were all together. Even though Nestaja couldn't drink, she excitedly turned her car around and headed downtown L.A. to enjoy a night with her girls.

Chapter 29

Some time had passed, and Nestaja was ready for S man's arrival the next day. The house in Arizona was ready and fully-furnished. She and Reggie sold the party business, and she hadn't heard from him since, nor had she heard from Vickie or Bayru since the party. It was like Craz had fallen off the planet, because she hadn't heard from him either.

Although she was enjoying their absences, she wanted to touch base with Bayru and Reggie, since she didn't want them popping up at the wrong time. She just needed to keep them away for a few days, because once S Man came home, they were scheduled to move shortly thereafter.

First, she called Asia to make sure she and the girls had made it to the motorcycle round-up in Atlanta safely. Then she decided to call Reggie, but she wasn't able to get him. She called Craz, but after he cursed her out and told her he moved on, she knew she didn't have to worry about him. She called Vickie, but talked to Ms. Doris and was informed that Vickie was shot with a .380 in the stomach. She had a colostomy bag and was still in the hospital. Bayru was shot in the shoulder and had surgery. He was also mourning Lil Bayru's and Roslind's deaths. Although she was a bit happy that she had hit Vickie without being noticed, she kinda felt bad that Bayru got tangled in his sister's web. He had no clue who Nestaja really was. Her guilt led her to call and check up on him.

"Hello?" he answered.

"I haven't heard from you. Just calling to make sure you a'ight."

"I got shot in my shoulder and I can't do much. If you're not doing anything in the morning, can you drive me to the pharmacy to get my pain medication, since you only live a few minutes away?" he asked.

"Well, I have somewhere to be tomorrow at 1:00 p.m.," she replied, hating that she called, because she wasn't going to let anything stop her from being on time to pick S Man up.

"Well, it will be ready at 7:00 in the morning and it's only about ten minutes away. I don't have anyone else to take me," he pitifully stated.

I haven't talked to this nigga in over a month, and now all of a sudden he needs me?

Where is the bitch that's been running for his ass? she thought. "I'll be there at 6:45, and I really don't have time to wait, so be ready," she sternly stated.

The next morning, her cousin Gina came by. She had stayed out with a friend and didn't want to drive home, and since Nestaja lived nearby, she went to her house to go to sleep. Nestaja was already up getting ready to take Bayru to the pharmacy, so she asked Gina to ride with her.

Without hesitation, Gina agreed. When they arrived, Gina let out a loud sigh. "What was that for?" Nestaja questioned.

"I'm so tired, cousin. I was up arguing with my friend all night," she answered nonchalantly.

When Bayru came out, he told Nestaja to drive his car. She agreed, because she really didn't want anyone to see him in hers. When they got to the stoplight on El Segundo and Avalon, Nestaja couldn't believe her eyes when she looked up and her eyes met with Reggie's, who was sitting in the driver's seat in the car next to them with a puzzled look on his face. A female sat on the passenger side. She looked over at Bayru, and when he noticed who was in the car next to them, she looked in the backseat at Gina, giving her the it's-about-to-go-down look.

Gina pulled her burner out, saying, "Nestaja, I can't let you do this to my man," referring to Bayru.

Nestaja already had her heater out on her lap. Just as she reached for it, Bayru reached for his and Reggie started busting. She managed to knock Bayru's gun from his hand, since he was fumbling with it with his bad one, and in the process, he was hit in the chest and instantly went into shock. When she looked back at Gina, she had already taken one of Reggie's bullets to the dome, so it was a wrap for her. She managed to get out of the car, but she held her heat in her hand, aiming at Reggie as she walked up to his car and opened the passenger door, forcing the female to climb in the back.

"Reggie, you better tell this bitch now that I'm your wife," the familiar raspy-voiced female said.

Even though Nestaja was blown away by her comment, she still got in the car, pushing the girl in the middle. She hated Reggie, but not enough to kill him, and he felt the same. He wasn't able to get at her like he wanted to because his wife was in the car.

"Just take me to my whip," Nestaja said as Reggie pulled off in a rage, causing the back tires on his car to burn rubber.

When she got to her car, she immediately got out of Dodge. Once she got home, she laid her head on the steering wheel and started crying.

"What have I done?" she yelled. "Gina is dead. I just had a shootout. And my man will be home in a few hours." After she sat in the car and cried for a little bit, she went inside and got ready to go get S man.

***

"Bayru, Blood, what took you so long to answer your phone? I seen that shit that went down with you and Jino's baby momma."

"Blood, if you seen the shit, why you didn't serve that nigga? I got hit in the chest and a nigga went out for a minute. If I didn't have my vest on, I would have went out for good, and I don't know Jino's baby momma," Bayru replied.

"Nigga, you was just in a shootout with that crab-ass bitch." "Who, Gina?" he questioned

"Nah, that Crip bitch you had driving your shit, Nestaja. But fuck all that. I followed the bitch. Jino dropped her off to her car, and she came home over here on 113th and Avalon. She just pulled out her driveway, nigga. I been calling you to see what you wanted me to do with her."

"Where she at now?" Bayru asked.

"I'm following her. She getting on the 110 freeway."

"Stay on her, and when you see me pull up, fall back and I'll take it from there," Bayru ordered.

***

Nestaja drove all the way to the prison, never noticing that she was being followed. When she saw S Man, she got out and greeted him. They were so happy to embrace each other, neither of them noticed the black car. S Man wanted to drive, so Nestaja got in the passenger seat and they hit the highway.

S Man got off the freeway after a few miles to get something to eat. When they got back on the freeway, he noticed that the same black car was still behind him, so he got off just to be sure. When the car got off too, he asked Nestaja, "Who the fuck is this nigga that's following us?"

When she looked back and noticed it was Bayru, she said to S Man, "I need to tell you something."

But before she could say anything, the car sped up and got on the side of them and riddled Nestaja's car with Mack 10 and .45 Magnum bullets.